OF MICE AND MEN

ACTING EDITION

★

PLAY IN THREE ACTS

BY JOHN STEINBECK

★

DRAMATISTS
PLAY SERVICE
INC.

This play was first presented by Sam H. Harris at the Music Box Theatre, New York, on November 23, 1937, with the following cast:

CAST OF CHARACTERS

GEORGE ....Wallace Ford
LENNIE ....Broderick Crawford
CANDY ....John F. Hamilton
THE BOSS ....Thomas Findlay
CURLEY ....Sam Byrd
CURLEY'S WIFE ....Claire Luce
SLIM ....Will Geer
CARLSON ....Charles Slattery
WHIT ....Walter Baldwin
CROOKS ....Leigh Whipper

Staged by GEORGE S. KAUFMAN

Settings by DONALD OENSLAGER

SYNOPSIS OF SCENES

ACT I

SCENE 1: A sandy bank of the Salinas River. Thursday night.
SCENE 2: The interior of a bunkhouse. Late Friday morning.

ACT 2

SCENE 1: The same as Act I—Scene 2. About seven-thirty Friday evening.
SCENE 2: The room of the stable buck, a lean-to. Ten o'clock Saturday evening.

ACT III

SCENE 1: One end of a great barn. Mid-afternoon, Sunday.
SCENE 2: Same as Act I—Scene 1. Sunday night.
TIME: The present.
PLACE: An agricultural valley in Northern California.

PRODUCTION NOTE

This is the first text of the play which may be considered in any sense an acting edition. For some years now OF MICE AND MEN has, even without an acting edition, or even without any text except in an anthology, proved continuously interesting to nonprofessional groups in the U. S. and many other countries.

This acting edition, while containing sufficient stage directions for general use, is not so detailed as many plays that require more realistic and exact instructions. The point is that the dialogue and characterization are in themselves so important as to render unnecessary the usual sort of stage directions in which every entrance is specifically referred to and almost every move of every character carefully designated. As a matter of fact, a good deal of the movement of the characters in nearly all the scenes can be left to a great extent to the discretion of the director. However, a few particular additional suggestions may be called for. These are as follows:

The outdoor scene (Act I—Scene 1 and Act III—Scene 1) needs almost no scenery. For example, the " sandy bank of the Salinas River " need actually show no trees whatsoever, and the river may be considered as flowing along the upper stretch of the stage. No attempt should be made at realism here. The author's description of this scene should be regarded not as a technical requirement but simply in order to set the mood. It may or may not be wise to show a little of the long grass mentioned in Act III—Scene 1. Much of this sort of thing not only can but should be left to the imagination. The same thing holds true with a good deal of the stage business here, such as the washing in the river and the drinking of water. It will, of course, occur to almost all directors that in Act I—Scene 1 and Act III—Scene 1, a good deal can be done by the discreet use of lights. Often a single spot on a particular bit of action will help in the preservation of the atmosphere aimed at.

Act I—Scene 2 is the interior of the bunkhouse. This scene has a single entrance, up c., which is used by all the actors in the scene. This should, of course, have a latch on it. At 'least one window is necessary upstage. This window should be arranged so that it can be opened and closed. The window should be fairly near the entrance. The main furniture required is the bunks, a few boxes and perhaps two or three occasional chairs; also small boxes nailed to the wall for each bunk. Finally, the hanging lamp from the ceiling, mentioned in the text. In this scene and in a later scene, it will be noticed that the old blind dog is described as actually on stage. Because getting and using an actual dog may offer real difficulties, the director is urged to consider some simple device whereby the dog is just offstage, at one side of the entrance. To do this will necessitate some slight alteration in the business of the scenes where the dog is now indicated as being actually on stage.

Act II—Scene 1. The tiny puppy referred to in this scene and the puppies referred to in other places throughout the play should not, of course, be real animals. A dummy or a roll of cloth can easily be substituted.

Act II—Scene 2. The setting here should be very small and compact, and dim lighting plays a most important part.

Act III—Scene 1. Although the actual playing space here is extremely small, it is supposed to be laid in a large barn. There is no point in attempting any sort of realistic presentation of the barn. As a matter of fact, all that is needed is a heap of hay down-stage c. The rest of the scene should be kept in shadow for the most part. Even the business of looking between the boards of the barn might be treated unrealistically, no actual sunlight coming in. It also makes little or no difference just from where the characters enter or where they go out.

Act III—Scene 2. Again the same setting as in Act I—Scene 1. Here the stage is almost in darkness at the beginning and at the end night has fallen.

It is suggested that when George shoots Lennie, the audience should see all the preparations for this, but the curtain might actually be down before we hear the shot.

OF MICE AND MEN

ACT I

SCENE 1

Thursday night. A sandy bank of the Salinas River sheltered with willows—one giant sycamore up R. The stage is covered with dry leaves. The feeling is sheltered and quiet. Stage is lit by a setting sun.

Curtain rises on empty stage. A sparrow is singing. There is a distant sound of ranch dogs barking aimlessly and one clear quail call. The quail call turns to a warning call and there is a beat of the flock's wings. Two figures are seen entering, L. or R., it makes no difference, in single file, with GEORGE, the short man, coming in ahead of LENNIE. Both men are carrying blanket rolls. They approach the water. The small man throws down his blanket roll, the large man follows, then falls down and drinks from the river, snorting as he drinks.[1]

GEORGE. (*Irritably.*) Lennie, for God's sake, don't drink so much. (*Leans over and shakes* LENNIE.) Lennie, you hear me! You gonna be sick like you was last night.

LENNIE. (*Dips his whole head under, hat and all. As he sits on bank, his hat drips down the back.*) That's good. You drink some, George. You drink some, too.

GEORGE. (*Kneeling, dipping his finger in water.*) I ain't sure it's good water. Looks kinda scummy to me.

LENNIE. (*Imitates, dipping his finger also.*) Look at them wrinkles in the water, George. Look what I done.

GEORGE. (*Drinking from his cupped palm.*) Tastes all right. Don't seem to be runnin' much, though. Lennie, you oughtn' to drink water when it ain't running. (*Hopelessly.*) You'd drink water out of a gutter if you was thirsty. (*Throws a scoop of water into his*

[1] See p. 5, *Production Note.*

face, rubs it around with his hand, pushes himself back and embraces his knees. LENNIE, *after watching him, imitates him in every detail.* GEORGE, *beginning tiredly and growing angry as he speaks.*) God damn it, we could just as well of rode clear to the ranch. That bus driver didn't know what he was talkin' about. " Just a little stretch down the highway," he says. " Just a little stretch "—damn near four miles! I bet he didn't want to stop at the ranch gate. . . . I bet he's too damn lazy to pull up. Wonder he ain't too lazy to stop at Soledad at all! (*Mumbling.*) Just a little stretch down the road.

LENNIE. (*Timidly.*) George?

GEORGE. Yeh . . . what you want?

LENNIE. Where we goin', George?

GEORGE. (*Jerks down his hat furiously.*) So you forgot that already, did you? So I got to tell you again! Jeez, you're crazy!

LENNIE. (*Softly.*) I forgot. I tried not to forget, honest to God, I did!

GEORGE. Okay, okay, I'll tell you again. . . . (*With sarcasm.*) I ain't got nothin' to do. Might just as well spen' all my time tellin' you things. You forgit 'em and I tell you again.

LENNIE. (*Continuing on from his last speech.*) I tried and tried, but it didn't do no good. I remember about the rabbits, George!

GEORGE. The hell with the rabbits! You can't remember nothing but them rabbits. You remember settin' in that gutter on Howard Street and watchin' that blackboard?

LENNIE. (*Delightedly.*) Oh, sure! I remember that . . . but . . . wha'd we do then? I remember some girls come by, and you says ——

GEORGE. The hell with what I says! You remember about us goin' in Murray and Ready's and they give us work cards and bus tickets?

LENNIE. (*Confidently.*) Oh, sure, George . . . I remember that now. (*Puts hand into side coat-pocket, his confidence vanishes. Very gently.*) . . . George?

GEORGE. Huh?

LENNIE. (*Staring at ground in despair.*) I ain't got mine. I musta lost it.

GEORGE. You never had none. I got both of 'em here. Think I'd let you carry your own work card?

LENNIE. (*With tremendous relief.*) I thought I put it in my side pocket. (*Puts hand in pocket again.*)

GEORGE. (*Looking sharply at him, and as he looks,* LENNIE *brings hand out of pocket.*) Wha'd you take out of that pocket?

LENNIE. (*Cleverly.*) Ain't a thing in my pocket.

GEORGE. I know there ain't. You got it in your hand now. What you got in your hand?

LENNIE. I ain't got nothing, George! Honest!

GEORGE. Come on, give it here!

LENNIE. (*Holds his closed hand away from* GEORGE.) It's on'y a mouse!

GEORGE. A mouse? A live mouse?

LENNIE. No . . . just a dead mouse. (*Worriedly.*) I didn't kill it. Honest. I found it. I found it dead.

GEORGE. Give it here!

LENNIE. Leave me have it, George.

GEORGE. (*Sternly.*) Give it here! (LENNIE *reluctantly gives him mouse.*) What do you want of a dead mouse, anyway?

LENNIE. (*In a propositional tone.*) I was petting it with my thumb while we walked along.

GEORGE. Well, you ain't pettin' no mice while you walk with me. Now let's see if you can remember where we're going. (GEORGE *throws it across the water into brush.*)

LENNIE. (*Looks startled, then in embarrassment hides his face against his knees.*) I forgot again.

GEORGE. Jesus Christ! (*Resignedly.*) Well, look, we are gonna work on a ranch like the one we come from up north.

LENNIE. Up north?

GEORGE. In Weed!

LENNIE. Oh, sure I remember—in Weed.

GEORGE. (*Still with exaggerated patience.*) That ranch we're goin' to is right down there about a quarter mile. We're gonna go in and see the boss.

LENNIE. (*Repeats, as a lesson.*) And see the boss!

GEORGE. Now, look! I'll give him the work tickets, but you ain't gonna say a word. You're just gonna stand there and not say nothing.

LENNIE. Not say nothing!

GEORGE. If he finds out what a crazy bastard you are, we won't get no job. But if he sees you work before he hears you talk, we're set. You got that?

LENNIE. Sure, George . . . sure. I got that.

GEORGE. Okay. Now when we go in to see the boss, what you gonna do?

LENNIE. (*Concentrating.*) I . . . I . . . I ain't gonna say nothing . . . jus' gonna stand there.

GEORGE. (*Greatly relieved.*) Good boy, that's swell! Now say that over two or three times so you sure won't forget it.

LENNIE. (*Drones softly under his breath.*) I ain't gonna say nothing . . . I ain't gonna say nothing. . . . (*Trails off into a whisper.*)

GEORGE. And you ain't gonna do no bad things like you done in Weed neither.

LENNIE. (*Puzzled.*) Like I done in Weed?

GEORGE. So you forgot that too, did you?

LENNIE. (*Triumphantly.*) They run us out of Weed!

GEORGE. (*Disgusted.*) Run us out, hell! We run! They was lookin' for us, but they didn't catch us.

LENNIE. (*Happily.*) I didn't forget that, you bet.

GEORGE. (*Lies back on sand, crosses hands under his head. Again* LENNIE *imitates him.*) God, you're a lot of trouble! I could get along so easy and nice, if I didn't have you on my tail. I could live so easy!

LENNIE. (*Hopefully.*) We gonna work on a ranch, George.

GEORGE. All right, you got that. But we're gonna sleep here tonight, because . . . I want to. I want to sleep out. (*The light is going fast, dropping into evening. A little wind whirls into the clearing and blows leaves. Dog howls in the distance.*)

LENNIE. Why ain't we goin' on to the ranch to get some supper? They got supper at the ranch.

GEORGE. No reason at all. I just like it here. Tomorrow we'll be goin' to work. I seen thrashing machines on the way down; that means we'll be buckin' grain bags. Bustin' a gut liftin' up them bags. Tonight I'm gonna lay right here an' look up! Tonight there ain't a grain bag or a boss in the world. Tonight, the drinks is on the . . . house. Nice house we got here, Lennie.

LENNIE. (*Gets up on his knees, looks down at* GEORGE, *plaintively.*) Ain't we gonna have no supper?

GEORGE. Sure we are. You gather up some dead willow sticks. I got three cans of beans in my bindle. I'll open 'em up while you get a fire ready. We'll eat 'em cold.

10

LENNIE. (*Companionably.*) I like beans with ketchup.

GEORGE. Well, we ain't got no ketchup. You go get wood, and don't you fool around none. Be dark before long. (LENNIE *lumbers to his feet and disappears into brush.* GEORGE *gets out bean cans, opens two, suddenly turns his head and listens. A little sound of splashing comes from direction that* LENNIE *has taken.* GEORGE *looks after him, shakes head.* LENNIE *comes back carrying a few small willow sticks.*) All right, give me that mouse.

LENNIE. (*With elaborate pantomime of innocence.*) What, George? I ain't got no mouse.

GEORGE. (*Holding out his hand.*) Come on! Give it to me! You ain't puttin' nothing over. (LENNIE *hesitates, backs away, turns and looks as if he were going to run. Coldly.*) You gonna give me that mouse or do I have to take a sock at you?

LENNIE. Give you what, George?

GEORGE. You know goddam well what! I want that mouse!

LENNIE. (*Almost in tears.*) I don't know why I can't keep it. It ain't nobody's mouse. I didn't steal it! I found it layin' right beside the road. (GEORGE *snaps fingers sharply, and* LENNIE *lays mouse in his hand.*) I wasn't doin' nothing bad with it. Just stroking it. That ain't bad.

GEORGE. (*Stands up, throws mouse as far as he can into the brush, then steps to pool, washes his hands.*) You crazy fool! Thought you could get away with it, didn't you? Don't you think I could see your feet was wet where you went in the water to get it? (LENNIE *whimpers like a puppy.*) Blubbering like a baby. Jesus Christ, a big guy like you! (LENNIE *tries to control himself, but his lips quiver and his face works with an effort.* GEORGE *puts hand on* LENNIE'S *shoulder for a moment.*) Aw, Lennie, I ain't takin' it away just for meanness. That mouse ain't fresh. Besides, you broke it pettin' it. You get a mouse that's fresh and I'll let you keep it a little while.

LENNIE. I don't know where there is no other mouse. I remember a lady used to give 'em to me. Ever' one she got she used to give it to me, but that lady ain't here no more.

GEORGE. Lady, huh! . . . Give me them sticks there. . . . Don't even remember who that lady was. That was your own Aunt Clara. She stopped givin' 'em to you. You always killed 'em.

LENNIE. (*Sadly, apologetically.*) They was so little. I'd pet 'em and pretty soon they bit my fingers and then I pinched their head a little bit and then they was dead . . . because they was so little. I wish we'd get the rabbits pretty soon, George. They ain't so little.

GEORGE. The hell with the rabbits! Come on, let's eat! (*The light has continued to go out of the scene so that when* GEORGE *lights fire, it is the major light.* GEORGE *hands an open can to* LENNIE.) There's enough beans for four men.

LENNIE. (*Sitting on other side of fire, speaks patiently.*) I like 'em with ketchup.

GEORGE. (*Explodes.*) Well, we ain't got any. Whatever we ain't got, that's what you want. God Almighty, if I was alone, I could live so easy. I could go get a job of work and no trouble. No mess . . . and when the end of the month come, I could take my fifty bucks and go into town and get whatever I want. Why, I could stay in a cat-house all night. I could eat any place I want. Order any damn thing.

LENNIE. (*Plaintively, but softly.*) I didn't want no ketchup.

GEORGE. (*Continuing violently.*) I could do that every damn month. Get a gallon of whiskey or set in a pool room and play cards or shoot pool. (LENNIE *gets up to his knees and looks over fire, with frightened face.*) And what have I got? (*Disgustedly.*) I got *you.* You can't keep a job and you lose me every job I get!

LENNIE. (*In terror.*) I don't mean nothing, George.

GEORGE. Just keep me shovin' all over the country all the time. And that ain't the worst—you get in trouble. You do bad things and I got to get you out. It ain't bad people that raises hell. It's dumb ones. (*Shouts.*) You crazy son-of-a-bitch, you keep me in hot water all the time. (LENNIE *is trying to stop* GEORGE'S *flow of words with his hands. Sarcastically.*) You just wanta feel that girl's dress. Just wanta pet it like it was a mouse. Well, how the hell'd she know you just wanta feel her dress? How'd she know you'd just hold onto it like it was a mouse?

LENNIE. (*In a panic.*) I didn't mean to, George!

GEORGE. Sure you didn't mean to. You didn't mean for her to yell bloody hell, either. You didn't mean for us to hide in the irrigation ditch all day with guys out lookin' for us with guns. Alla time it's something you didn't mean. God damn it, I wish I could put you in a cage with a million mice and let them pet *you.* (GEORGE'S *anger leaves him suddenly. For the first time he seems to see the expression of terror on* LENNIE'S *face. Looks ashamedly at fire, and maneuvers some beans onto blade of his pocket-knife, puts them into his mouth.)*

LENNIE. *(After a pause.)* George! (GEORGE *purposely does not answer him.)* George?

GEORGE. What do you want?

LENNIE. I was only foolin', George. I don't want no ketchup. I wouldn't eat no ketchup if it was right here beside me.

GEORGE. *(With a sullenness of shame.)* If they was some here you could have it. And if I had a thousand bucks I'd buy ya a bunch of flowers.

LENNIE. I wouldn't eat no ketchup, George. I'd leave it all for you. You could cover your beans so deep with it, and I wouldn't touch none of it.

GEORGE. *(Refusing to give in from his sullenness, refusing to look at* LENNIE.) When I think of the swell time I could have without you, I go nuts. I never git no peace!

LENNIE. You want I should go away and leave you alone?

GEORGE. Where the hell could you go?

LENNIE. Well, I could . . . I could go off in the hills there Some place I could find a cave.

GEORGE. Yeah, how'd ya eat? You ain't got sense enough to find nothing to eat.

LENNIE. I'd find things. I don't need no nice food with ketchup. I'd lay out in the sun and nobody would hurt me. And if I found a mouse—why, I could keep it. Wouldn't nobody take it away from me.

GEORGE. *(At last looks up.)* I been mean, ain't I?

LENNIE. *(Presses his triumph.)* If you don't want me, I can go right in them hills, and find a cave. I can go away any time.

GEORGE. No. Look! I was just foolin' ya. 'Course I want you to stay with me. Trouble with mice is you always kill 'em. *(Pauses.)* Tell you what I'll do, Lennie. First chance I get I'll find you a pup. Maybe you wouldn't kill it. That would be better than mice. You could pet it harder.

LENNIE. *(Still avoiding being drawn in.)* If you don't want me, you only gotta say so. I'll go right up on them hills and live by myself. And I won't get no mice stole from me.

GEORGE. I want you to stay with me. Jesus Christ, somebody'd shoot you for a coyote if you was by yourself. Stay with me.

Your Aunt Clara wouldn't like your runnin' off by yourself, even if she is dead.

LENNIE. George?

GEORGE. Huh?

LENNIE. (*Craftily.*) Tell me—like you done before.

GEORGE. Tell you what?

LENNIE. About the rabbits.

GEORGE. (*Near to anger again.*) You ain't gonna put nothing over on me!

LENNIE. (*Pleading.*) Come on, George . . . tell me! Please! Like you done before.

GEORGE. You get a kick out of that, don't you? All right, I'll tell you. And then we'll lay out our beds and eat our dinner.

LENNIE. Go on, George. (*Unrolls his bed and lies on his side, supporting his head on one hand.* GEORGE *lays out his bed, sits crosslegged on it.* GEORGE *repeats next speech rhythmically, as though he had said it many times before.*)

GEORGE. Guys like us that work on ranches is the loneliest guys in the world. They ain't got no family. They don't belong no place. They come to a ranch and work up a stake and then they go in to town and blow their stake. And then the first thing you know they're poundin' their tail on some other ranch. They ain't got nothin' to look ahead to.

LENNIE. (*Delightedly.*) That's it, that's it! Now tell how it is with us.

GEORGE. (*Still almost chanting.*) With us it ain't like that. We got a future. We got somebody to talk to that gives a damn about us. We don't have to sit in no barroom blowin' in our jack, just because we got no place else to go. If them other guys gets in jail, they can rot for all anybody gives a damn.

LENNIE. (*Who cannot restrain himself any longer. Bursts into speech.*) But not us! And why? Because . . . because I got you to look after me . . . . and you got me to look after you . . . and that's why! (*He laughs.*) Go on, George!

GEORGE. You got it by heart. You can do it yourself.

LENNIE. No, no. I forget some of the stuff. Tell about how it's gonna be.

GEORGE. Some other time.

LENNIE. No, tell how it's gonna be!

GEORGE. Okay. Some day we're gonna get the jack together and we're gonna have a little house, and a couple of acres and a cow and some pigs and . . .

LENNIE. (*Shouting.*) And live off the fat of the land! And have rabbits. Go on, George! Tell about what we're gonna have in the garden. And about the rabbits in the cages. Tell about the rain in the winter . . . and about the stove and how thick the cream is on the milk, you can hardly cut it. Tell about that, George!

GEORGE. Why don't you do it yourself—you know all of it!

LENNIE. It ain't the same if I tell it. Go on now. How I get to tend the rabbits.

GEORGE. (*Resignedly.*) Well, we'll have a big vegetable patch and a rabbit hutch and chickens. And when it rains in the winter we'll just say to hell with goin' to work. We'll build up a fire in the stove, and set around it and listen to the rain comin' down on the roof —— Nuts! (*Begins to eat with his knife.*) I ain't got time for no more. (*Falls to eating.* LENNIE *imitates him, spilling a few beans from his mouth with every bite.* GEORGE, *gesturing with knife.*) What you gonna say tomorrow when the boss asks you questions?

LENNIE. (*Stops chewing in middle of a bite, swallows painfully. His face contorts with thought.*) I . . . I ain't gonna say a word.

GEORGE. Good boy. That's fine. Say, maybe you're gittin' better. I bet I can let you tend the rabbits . . . specially if you remember as good as that!

LENNIE. (*Choking with pride.*) I can remember, by God!

GEORGE. (*As though remembering, points knife at* LENNIE'S *chest.*) Lennie, I want you to look around here. Think you can remember this place? The ranch is 'bout a quarter mile up that way. Just follow the river and you can get here.

LENNIE. (*Looking around carefully.*) Sure, I can remember here. Didn't I remember 'bout not gonna say a word?

GEORGE. 'Course you did. Well, look, Lennie, if you just happen to get in trouble, I want you to come right here and hide in the brush.

LENNIE. (*Slowly.*) Hide in the brush.

GEORGE. Hide in the brush until I come for you. Think you can remember that?

LENNIE. Sure I can, George. Hide in the brush till you come for me!

GEORGE. But you ain't gonna get in no trouble. Because if you do I won't let you tend the rabbits.

LENNIE. I won't get in no trouble. I ain't gonna say a word.

GEORGE. You got it. Anyways, I hope so. (GEORGE *stretches out on his blankets. Light dies slowly out of the fire until only the faces of the two men can be seen.* GEORGE *is still eating from his can of beans.*) It's gonna be nice sleeping here. Lookin' up . . . and the leaves . . . Don't build up no more fire. We'll let her die. Jesus, you feel free when you ain't got a job—if you ain't hungry. (*They sit silently a few moments. A night owl is heard far off. From across river the sound of a coyote howl and on the heels of a howl all the dogs in the country start to bark.*)

LENNIE. (*From almost complete darkness.*) George?

GEORGE. What do you want?

LENNIE. Let's have different color rabbits, George.

GEORGE. Sure. Red rabbits and blue rabbits and green rabbits. Millions of 'em!

LENNIE. Furry ones, George. Like I seen at the fair in Sacramento.

GEORGE. Sure. Furry ones.

LENNIE. 'Cause I can jus' as well go away, George, and live in a cave.

GEORGE. (*Amiably.*) Aw, shut up.

LENNIE. (*After long pause.*) George?

GEORGE. What is it?

LENNIE. I'm shutting up, George. (*Coyote howls again.*)

CURTAIN

ACT I

Scene 2

Late Friday morning. Interior of a bunkhouse. Walls, white-washed board and bat. Floors unpainted. A heavy square table C. *with upended boxes around it used for chairs. Over each bunk there is a box nailed to the wall, which serves as two shelves on which are the private possessions of the working men. On top of each bunk a large alarm clock ticking madly. A box or two, or*

16

three, here and there, which can on occasion be used for chairs. *The sun is streaking through the windows, U. C. One or two others may be used as needed.* NOTE: *Articles in boxes on wall are soap, talcum powder, razors, pulp magazines, medicine bottles, combs, and from nails on the sides of the boxes a few neckties. A hanging light from ceiling over table, with a round dim reflector on it.*

Curtain rises on an empty stage. Only the ticking of the many clocks is heard. CANDY, GEORGE *and* LENNIE *are first seen passing open window U. C.*

CANDY. This is the bunkhouse here. Door's around this side. (*Latch on door C. rises and* CANDY *enters, a stoop-shouldered old man, dressed in blue-jeans and denim coat. Carries a big push broom in his L. hand. His R. hand is gone at the wrist. Grasps things with his R. arm between arm and side. Walks into room, followed by* GEORGE *and* LENNIE. *Conversationally.*) The boss was expecting you last night. He was sore as hell when you wasn't here to go out this morning. (*Points with handless arm.*) You can have them two beds there.

GEORGE. I'll take the top one . . . I don't want you falling down on me. (*Steps over to one of the bunks, throws his blankets down. Looks into nearly empty box shelf over it, then picks up a small yellow can.*) Say, what the hell's this?

CANDY. I don' know.

GEORGE. Says " positively kills lice, roaches and other scourges." What the hell kinda beds you givin' us, anyway? We don't want no pants rabbits.

CANDY. (*Shifts broom, holding it between his elbow and his side, takes can in L. hand, studies label carefully.*) Tell you what . . . last guy that had this bed was a blacksmith. Helluva nice fellow. Clean a guy as you'd want to meet. Used to wash his hands even *after* he et.

GEORGE. (*With gathering anger.*) Then how come he got pillow-pigeons? (LENNIE *puts his blankets on bunk and sits down, watching* GEORGE *with his mouth slightly open.*)

CANDY. Tell you what. This here blacksmith, name of Whitey, was the kinda guy that would put that stuff around even if there wasn't no bugs. Tell you what he used to do. He'd peel *his* boiled potatoes and take out every little spot before he et it, and if there was a red splotch on an egg, he'd scrape it off. Finally quit about the food. That's the kind of guy Whitey was. Clean. Used to dress up Sundays even when he wasn't goin' no place. Put on a necktie even, and then set in the bunkhouse.

GEORGE. (*Skeptically*.) I ain't so sure. What da' ya say he quit for?

CANDY. (*Puts can in pocket, rubs his whiskers with knuckles*.) Why . . . he just quit the way a guy will. Says it was the food. Didn't give no other reason. Just says "give me my time" one night, the way any guy would. (GEORGE *lifts his bed tick and looks underneath, leans over, inspects sacking carefully.* LENNIE *does same with his bed*.)

GEORGE. (*Half satisfied*.) Well, if there's any gray-backs in this bed, you're gonna hear from me! (*Unrolls blankets and puts his razor, soap, comb, bottle of pills, liniment and leather wristband in box*.)

CANDY. I guess the boss'll be out here in a minute to write your name in. He sure was burned when you wasn't here this morning. Come right in when we was eatin' breakfast and says, "Where the hell's them new men?" He give the stable buck hell, too. Stable buck's a nigger.

GEORGE. Nigger, huh!

CANDY. Yeah. (*Continues*.) Nice fellow, too. Got a crooked back where a horse kicked him. Boss gives him hell when he's mad. But the stable buck don't give a damn about that.

GEORGE. What kinda guy is the boss?

CANDY. Well, he's a pretty nice fella for a boss. Gets mad sometimes. But he's pretty nice. Tell you what. Know what he done Christmas? Brung a gallon of whiskey right in here and says, "Drink hearty, boys, Christmas comes but once a year!"

GEORGE. The hell he did! A whole gallon?

CANDY. Yes, sir. Jesus, we had fun! They let the nigger come in that night. Well, sir, a little skinner name Smitty took after the nigger. Done pretty good too. The guys wouldn't let him use his feet so the nigger got him. If he could a used his feet Smitty says he would have killed the nigger. The guys says on account the nigger got a crooked back Smitty can't use his feet. (*Smiles in reverie at memory*.)

GEORGE. Boss the owner?

CANDY. Naw! Superintendent. Big land company. . . . Yes, sir, that night . . . he come right in here with a whole gallon . . . he set right over there and says, "Drink hearty, boys," . . . he says. . . . (*Door opens. Enter the* BOSS, *a stock man, dressed in blue-jean trousers, flannel shirt, black unbuttoned vest and black coat. Wears soiled brown Stetson hat, a pair of high-heeled boots and spurs. Ordinarily he puts his thumbs in his belt.* CANDY, *shuffling towards door, rubbing his whiskers with his knuckles as he goes.*) Them guys just come. (CANDY *exits shuts door behind him.*)

BOSS. I wrote Murray and Ready I wanted two men this morning. You got your work slips?

GEORGE. (*Digs in his pockets, produces two slips, hands them to* BOSS.) Here they are.

BOSS. (*Reading slips.*) Well, I see it wasn't Murray and Ready's fault. It says right here on the slip, you was to be here for work this morning.

GEORGE. Bus driver give us a bum steer. We had to walk ten miles. That bus driver says we was here when we wasn't. We couldn't thumb no rides. (GEORGE *scowls meaningly at* LENNIE, *who nods to show that he understands.*)

BOSS. Well, I had to send out the grain teams short two buckers. It won't do any good to go out now until after dinner. You'd get lost. (*Pulls out time book, opens it to where pencil is stuck between leaves. Licks pencil carefully.*) What's your name?

GEORGE. George Milton.

BOSS. George Milton. (*Writing.*) And what's yours?

GEORGE. His name's Lennie Small.

BOSS. Lennie Small. (*Writing.*) Le's see, this is the twentieth. Noon the twentieth. . . . (*Makes positive mark. Closes book, puts it in pocket.*) Where you boys been workin'?

GEORGE. Up around Weed.

BOSS. (*To* LENNIE.) You too?

GEORGE. Yeah. Him too.

BOSS. (*To* LENNIE.) Say, you're a big fellow, ain't you?

GEORGE. Yeah, he can work like hell, too.

BOSS. He ain't much of a talker, though, is he?

GEORGE. No, he ain't. But he's a hell of a good worker. Strong as a bull.

LENNIE. (*Smiling.*) I'm strong as a bull. (GEORGE *scowls at him,*

LENNIE *drops head in shame at having forgotten.*)

BOSS. (*Sharply.*) You are, huh? What can you do?

GEORGE. He can do anything.

BOSS. (*Addressing* LENNIE.) What can you do? (LENNIE, *looking at* GEORGE, *gives a high nervous chuckle.*)

GEORGE. (*Quickly.*) Anything you tell him. He's a good skinner. He can wrestle grain bags, drive a cultivator. He can do anything. Just give him a try.

BOSS. (*Turning to* GEORGE.) Then why don't you let *him* answer? (LENNIE *laughs.*) What's he laughing about?

GEORGE. He laughs when he gets excited.

BOSS. Yeah?

GEORGE. (*Loudly.*) But he's a goddamn good worker. I ain't saying he's bright, because he ain't. But he can put up a four hundred pound bale.

BOSS. (*Hooking his thumbs in his belt.*) Say, what you sellin'?

GEORGE. Huh?

BOSS. I said what stake you got in this guy? You takin' his pay away from him?

GEORGE. No. Of course I ain't!

BOSS. Well, I never seen one guy take so much trouble for another guy. I just like to know what your percentage is.

GEORGE. He's my . . . cousin. I told his ole lady I'd take care of him. He got kicked in the head by a horse when he was a kid. He's all right. . . . Just ain't bright. But he can do anything you tell him.

BOSS. (*Turning half away.*) Well, God knows he don't need no brains to buck barley bags. (*Turns back.*) But don't you try to put nothing over, Milton. I got my eye on you. Why'd you quit in Weed?

GEORGE. (*Promptly.*) Job was done.

BOSS. What kind of job?

GEORGE. Why . . . we was diggin' a cesspool.

BOSS. (*After a pause.*) All right. But don't try to put nothing over 'cause you can't get away with nothing. I seen wise guys before. Go out with the grain teams after dinner. They're out pickin' up barley with the thrashin' machines. Go out with Slim's team.

GEORGE. Slim?

BOSS. Yeah. Big, tall skinner. You'll see him at dinner. (*Up to this time the* BOSS *has been full of business, calm and suspicious.*

20

In following lines he relaxes, but gradually, as though he wanted to talk but felt the burden of his position. Turns toward door, u. c., but hesitates and allows a little warmth into his manner.) Been on the road long?

GEORGE. *(Obviously on guard.)* We was three days in 'Frisco lookin' at the boards.

BOSS. *(With heavy jocularity.)* Didn't go to no night clubs, I s'pose?

GEORGE. *(Stiffly.)* We was lookin' for a job.

BOSS. *(Attempting to be friendly.)* That's a great town if you got a little jack, Frisco.

GEORGE. *(Refusing to be drawn in.)* We didn't have no jack for nothing like that.

BOSS. *(Realizes there is no contact to establish, grows rigid with his position again.)* Go out with the grain teams after dinner. When my hands work hard they get pie and when they loaf they bounce down the road on their can. You ask anybody about me. *(Turns, walks out.)*

GEORGE. *(Turns to* LENNIE.*)* So you wasn't gonna say a word! You was gonna leave your big flapper shut. I was gonna do the talkin'. . . . You goddamn near lost us the job!

LENNIE. *(Stares hopelessly at hands.)* I forgot.

GEORGE. You forgot. You always forget. Now, he's got his eye on us. Now, we gotta be careful and not make no slips. You keep your big flapper shut after this.

LENNIE. He talked like a kinda nice guy towards the last.

GEORGE. *(Angrily.)* He's the boss, ain't he? Well, he's the boss first an' a nice guy afterwards. Don't you have nothin' to do with no boss, except do your work and draw your pay. You can't never tell whether you're talkin' to the nice guy or the boss. Just keep your goddamn mouth shut. Then you're all right.

LENNIE. George?

GEORGE. What you want now?

LENNIE. I wasn't kicked in the head with no horse, was I, George?

GEORGE. Be a damn good thing if you was. Save everybody a hell of a lot of trouble!

LENNIE. *(Flattered.)* You says I was your cousin.

GEORGE. Well, that was a goddamn lie. And I'm glad it was. Why, if I was a relative of yours —— *(Stops and listens, then steps to front door, looks out.)* Say, what the hell you doin', listenin'?

CANDY. (*Comes slowly into room. By a rope, he leads an ancient drag-footed blind sheep dog.*[1] *Sits on box, presses hind quarters of dog down.*) Naw . . . I wasn't listenin'. . . . I was just standin' in the shade a minute, scratchin' my dog. I jest now finished swamping out the washhouse.

GEORGE. You was pokin' your big nose into our business! I don't like nosey guys.

CANDY. (*Looks uneasily from* GEORGE *to* LENNIE, *then back.*) I jest come there . . . I didn't hear nothing you guys was sayin'. I ain't interested in nothing you was sayin'. A guy on a ranch don't never listen. Nor he don't ast no questions.

GEORGE. (*Slightly mollified.*) Damn right he don't! Not if the guy wants to stay workin' long. (*Manner changes.*) That's a helluva ole dog.

CANDY. Yeah. I had him ever since he was a pup. God, he was a good sheep dog, when he was young. (*Rubs cheek with knuckles.*) How'd you like the boss?

GEORGE. Pretty good! Seemed all right.

CANDY. He's a nice fella. You got ta take him right, of course. He's runnin' this ranch. He don't take no nonsense.

GEORGE. What time do we eat? Eleven-thirty? (CURLEY *enters, dressed in working clothes. Wears brown high-heeled boots and has a glove on his* L. *hand.*)

CURLEY. Seen my ole man?

CANDY. He was here just a minute ago, Curley. Went over to the cookhouse, I think.

CURLEY. I'll try to catch him. (*Looking at the new men, measuring them. Unconsciously bends his elbows, closes his hand, and goes into a slight crouch. Walks gingerly close to* LENNIE.) You the new guys my ole man was waitin' for?

GEORGE. Yeah. We just come in.

CURLEY. How's it come you wasn't here this morning?

GEORGE. Got off the bus too soon.

CURLEY. (*Again addressing* LENNIE.) My ole man got to get the grain out. Ever bucked barley?

GEORGE. (*Quickly.*) Hell, yes. Done a lot of it.

CURLEY. I mean him. (*To* LENNIE.) Ever bucked barley?

GEORGE. Sure he has.

CURLEY. (*Irritatedly.*) Let the big buy talk!

[1] See p. 5, Production Note.

22

GEORGE. S'pose he don't want ta talk?

CURLEY. (*Pugnaciously.*) By Christ, he's gotta talk when he's spoke to. What the hell you shovin' into this for?

GEORGE. (*Stands up, speaks coldly.*) Him and me travel together.

CURLEY. Oh, so it's that way?

GEORGE. (*Tense and motionless.*) What way?

CURLEY. (*Letting subject drop.*) And you won't let the big guy talk? Is that it?

GEORGE. He can talk if he wants to tell you anything. (*Nods slightly to* LENNIE.)

LENNIE. (*In a frightened voice.*) We just come in.

CURLEY. Well, next time you answer when you're spoke to, then.

GEORGE. He didn't do nothing to you.

CURLEY. (*Measuring him.*) You drawin' cards this hand?

GEORGE. (*Quietly.*) I might.

CURLEY. (*Stares at him a moment, his threat moving to the future.*) I'll see you get a chance to ante, anyway. (*Walks out of room.*)

GEORGE. (*After* CURLEY *leaves.*) Say, what the hell's he got on his shoulder? Lennie didn't say nothing to him.

CANDY. (*Looks cautiously at door.*) That's the boss's son. Curley's pretty handy. He done quite a bit in the ring. The guys say he's pretty handy.

GEORGE. Well, let 'im be handy. He don't have to take after Lennie. Lennie didn't do nothing to him.

CANDY. (*Considering.*) Well . . . tell you what, Curley's like a lot a little guys. He hates big guys. He's alla time pickin' scraps with big guys. Kinda like he's mad at 'em because he ain't a big guy. You seen little guys like that, ain't you—always scrappy?

GEORGE. Sure, I seen plenty tough little guys. But this here Curley better not make no mistakes about Lennie. Lennie ain't handy, see, but this Curley punk's gonna get hurt if he messes around with Lennie.

CANDY. (*Skeptically.*) Well, Curley's pretty handy. You know, it never did seem right to me. S'pose Curley jumps a big guy and licks him. Everybody says what a game guy Curley is. Well, s'pose he jumps 'im and gits licked, everybody says the big guy oughta pick somebody his own size. Seems like Curley ain't givin' nobody a chance.

GEORGE. (*Watching door.*) Well, he better watch out for Lennie.

Lennie ain't no fighter. But Lennie's strong and quick and Lennie don't know no rules. (*Walks to table, sits on box near it. Picks up scattered cards, pulls them together, shuffles them.*)

CANDY. Don't tell Curley I said none of this. He'd slough me! He jus' don't give a damn. Won't ever get canned because his ole man's the boss!

GEORGE. (*Cuts cards. Turns over and looks at each as he throws it down.*) This guy Curley sounds like a son-of-a-bitch to me! I don't like mean little guys!

CANDY. Seems to me like he's worse lately. He got married a couple of weeks ago. Wife lives over in the boss's house. Seems like Curley's worse'n ever since he got married. Like he's settin' on a ant-hill an' a big red ant come up an' nipped 'im on the turnip. Just feels so goddam miserable he'll strike at anything that moves. I'm kinda sorry for 'im.

GEORGE. Maybe he's showin' off for his wife.

CANDY. You seen that glove on his left hand?

GEORGE. Sure I seen it!

CANDY. Well, that glove's full of vaseline.

GEORGE. Vaseline? What the hell for?

CANDY. Curley says he's keepin' that hand soft for his wife.

GEORGE. That's a dirty kind of a thing to tell around.

CANDY. I ain't quite so sure. I seen such funny things a guy will do to try to be nice. I ain't sure. But you jus' wait till you see Curley's wife!

GEORGE. (*Begins to lay out a solitaire hand, speaks casually.*) Is she purty?

CANDY. Yeah. Purty, but ——

GEORGE. (*Studying cards.*) But what?

CANDY. Well, she got the eye.

GEORGE. (*Still playing his solitaire hand.*) Yeah? Married two weeks an' got the eye? Maybe that's why Curley's pants is fulla ants.

CANDY. Yes, sir, I seen her give Slim the eye. Slim's a jerk-line skinner. Hell of a nice fella. Well, I seen her give Slim the eye. Curley never seen it. And I seen her give a skinner named Carlson the eye.

GEORGE. (*Pretending very mild interest.*) Looks like we was gonna have fun!

CANDY. (*Stands up.*) Know what I think? (*Waits for answer.*

24

GEORGE *doesn't answer*.) Well, I think Curley's married himself a tart.

GEORGE. (*Casually*.) He ain't the first. Black queen on a red king. Yes, sir . . . there's plenty done that!

CANDY. (*Moves toward door, leading dog out with him*.) I got to be settin' out the wash basins for the guys. The teams'll be in before long. You guys gonna buck barley?

GEORGE. Yeah.

CANDY. You won't tell Curley nothing I said?

GEORGE. Hell, no!

CANDY. (*Just before he goes out, he turns back*.) Well, you look her over, Mister. You see if she ain't a tart! (*He exits*.)

GEORGE. (*Continuing to play out solitaire. Turns to* LENNIE.) Look, Lennie, this here ain't no set-up. You gonna have trouble with that Curley guy. I seen that kind before. You know what he's doin'. He's kinda feelin' you out. He figures he's got you scared. And he's gonna take a sock at you, first chance he gets.

LENNIE. (*Frightened*.) I don't want no trouble. Don't let him sock me, George!

GEORGE. I hate them kind of bastards. I seen plenty of 'em. Like the ole guy says: " Curley don't take no chances. He always figures to win." (*Thinks a moment*.) If he tangles with you, Lennie, we're goin' get the can. Don't make no mistake about that. He's the boss's kid. Look, you try to keep away from him, will you? Don't never speak to him. If he comes in here you move clear to the other side of the room. Will you remember that, Lennie?

LENNIE. (*Mourning*.) I don't want no trouble. I never done nothing to him!

GEORGE. Well, that won't do you no good, if Curley wants to set himself up for a fighter. Just don't have nothing to do with him. Will you remember?

LENNIE. Sure, George . . . I ain't gonna say a word. (*Sounds of teams coming in from the fields, jingling of harness, croak of heavy laden axles, men talking to and cussing horses. Crack of a whip and from a distance a voice calling*.)

SLIM'S VOICE. Stable buck! Stable buck! Hey! Stable buck!

GEORGE. Here come the guys. Just don't say nothing.

LENNIE. (*Timidly*.) You ain't mad, George?

GEORGE. I ain't mad at you. I'm mad at this here Curley bastard!

I wanted we should get a little stake together. Maybe a hundred dollars. You keep away from Curley.

LENNIE. Sure I will. I won't say a word.

GEORGE. (*Hesitating.*) Don't let 'im pull you in—but—if the son-of-a-bitch socks you—let him have it!

LENNIE. Let him have what, George?

GEORGE. Never mind. . . . Look, if you get in any kind of trouble, you remember what I told you to do.

LENNIE. If I get in any trouble, you ain't gonna let me tend the rabbits?

GEORGE. That's not what I mean. You remember where we slept last night. Down by the river?

LENNIE. Oh, sure I remember. I go there and hide in the brush until you come for me.

GEORGE. That's it. Hide till I come for you. Don't let nobody see you. Hide in the brush by the river. Now say that over.

LENNIE. Hide in the brush by the river. Down in the brush by the river.

GEORGE. If you get in trouble.

LENNIE. If I get in trouble. (*A brake screeches outside and a call: " Stable buck, oh, stable buck!" Suddenly* CURLEY'S WIFE *is standing in* C. *door. Full, heavily rouged lips. Wide-spaced, made-up eyes, her fingernails are bright red, hair hangs in little rolled clusters like sausages. Wears a cotton house dress and red mules, on the insteps of which are little bouquets of red ostrich feathers.* GEORGE *and* LENNIE *look up at her.*)

CURLEY'S WIFE. I'm lookin' for Curley!

GEORGE. (*Looks away from her.*) He was in here a minute ago but he went along.

CURLEY'S WIFE. (*Puts hands behind back, leans against door frame so that her body is thrown forward.*) You're the new fellas that just come, ain't you?

GEORGE. (*Sullenly.*) Yeah.

CURLEY'S WIFE. (*Bridles a little, inspects her fingernails.*) Sometimes Curley's in here.

GEORGE. (*Brusquely.*) Well, he ain't now!

CURLEY'S WIFE. (*Playfully.*) Well, if he ain't, I guess I'd better look some place else. (LENNIE *watches her, fascinated.*)

GEORGE. If I see Curley I'll pass the word you was lookin' for him.

CURLEY'S WIFE. Nobody can't blame a person for lookin'.

GEORGE. That depends what she's lookin' for.

CURLEY'S WIFE. (*A little wearily, dropping coquetry.*) I'm jus' lookin' for somebody to talk to. Don't you never jus' want to talk to somebody?

SLIM. (*Offstage.*) Okay! Put that lead pair in the north stalls.

CURLEY'S WIFE. (*To* SLIM, *offstage.*) Hi, Slim!

SLIM. (*Voice offstage.*) Hello.

CURLEY'S WIFE. I—I'm tryin' to find Curley.

SLIM'S VOICE. (*Offstage.*) Well, you ain't tryin' very hard. I seen him goin' in your house.

CURLEY'S WIFE. (*Turning back toward* GEORGE *and* LENNIE.) I gotta be goin'! (*She exits hurriedly.*)

GEORGE. (*Looking around at* LENNIE.) Jesus, what a tramp! So that's what Curley picks for a wife. God Almighty, did you smell that stink she's got on? I can still smell her. Don't have to see *her* to know she's around.

LENNIE. She's purty!

GEORGE. Yeah. And she's sure hidin' it. Curley got his work ahead of him.

LENNIE. (*Still staring at doorway where she was.*) Gosh, she's purty!

GEORGE. (*Turning furiously at him.*) Listen to me, you crazy bastard. Don't you even look at that bitch. I don't care what she says or what she does. I seen 'em poison before, but I ain't never seen no piece of jail bait worse than her. Don't you even smell near her!

LENNIE. I never smelled, George!

GEORGE. No, you never. But when she was standin' there showin' her legs, you wasn't lookin' the other way neither!

LENNIE. I never meant no bad things, George. Honest I never.

GEORGE. Well, you keep away from her. You let Curley take the rap. He let himself in for it. (*Disgustedly.*) Glove full of vaseline. I bet he's eatin' raw eggs and writin' to patent-medicine houses.

LENNIE. (*Cries out.*) I don't like this place. This ain't no good place. I don't like this place!

GEORGE. Listen—I don't like it here no better than you do. But we gotta keep it till we get a stake. We're flat. We gotta get a stake. (*Goes back to table, thoughtfully.*) If we can get just a few dollars in the poke we'll shove off and go up to the American River and pan gold. Guy can make a couple dollars a day there.

LENNIE. (*Eagerly.*) Let's go, George. Let's get out of here. It's mean here.

GEORGE. (*Shortly.*) I tell you we gotta stay a little while. We gotta get a stake. (*Sounds of running water and rattle of basins are heard.*) Shut up now, the guys'll be comin' in! (*Pensively.*) Maybe we ought to wash up. . . . But hell, we ain't done nothin' to get dirty.

SLIM. (*Enters C. He is a tall, dark man in blue-jeans and short denim jacket. Carries a crushed Stetson hat under his arm and combs his long dark damp hair straight back. Stands and moves with a kind of majesty. Finishes combing his hair. Smooths out his crushed hat, creases it in the middle and puts it on. In a gentle voice.*) It's brighter'n a bitch outside. Can't hardly see nothing in here. You the new guys?

GEORGE. Just come.

SLIM. Goin' to buck barley?

GEORGE. That's what the boss says.

SLIM. Hope you get on my team.

GEORGE. Boss said we'd go with a jerk-line skinner named Slim.

SLIM. That's me.

GEORGE. You a jerk-line skinner?

SLIM. (*In self-disparagement.*) I can snap 'em around a little.

GEORGE. (*Terribly impressed.*) That kinda makes you Jesus Christ on this ranch, don't it?

SLIM. (*Obviously pleased.*) Oh, nuts!

GEORGE. (*Chuckles.*) Like the man says, " The boss tells you what to do. But if you want to know how to do it, you got to ask the mule skinner." The man says any guy that can drive twelve Arizona jack rabbits with a jerk line can fall in a toilet and come up with a mince pie under each arm.

SLIM. (*Laughing.*) Well, I hope you get on my team. I got a pair a punks that don't know a barley bag from a blue ball. You guys ever bucked any barley?

GEORGE. Hell, yes. I ain't nothin' to scream about, but that big guy there can put up more grain alone than most pairs can.

SLIM. (*Looks approvingly at* GEORGE.) You guys travel around together?

GEORGE. Sure. We kinda look after each other. (*Points at* LENNIE *with thumb.*) He ain't bright. Hell of a good worker, though. Hell of a nice fella too. I've knowed him for a long time.

SLIM. Ain't many guys travel around together. I don't know why. Maybe everybody in the whole damn world is scared of each other.

GEORGE. It's a lot nicer to go 'round with a guy you know. You get used to it an' then it ain't no fun alone any more. (*Enter* CARLSON. *Big-stomached, powerful. His head still drips water from scrubbing and dousing.*)

CARLSON. Hello, Slim! (*Looks at* GEORGE *and* LENNIE.)

SLIM. These guys just come.

CARLSON. Glad to meet ya! My name's Carlson.

GEORGE. I'm George Milton. This here's Lennie Small.

CARLSON. Glad to meet you. He ain't very small. (*Chuckles at his own joke.*) He ain't small at all. Meant to ask you, Slim, how's your bitch? I seen she wasn't under your wagon this morning.

SLIM. She slang her pups last night. Nine of 'em. I drowned four of 'em right off. She couldn't feed that many.

CARLSON. Got five left, huh?

SLIM. Yeah. Five. I kep' the biggest.

CARLSON. What kinda dogs you think they gonna be?

SLIM. I don't know. Some kind of shepherd, I guess. That's the most kind I seen around here when she's in heat.

CARLSON. (*Laughs.*) I had an airedale an' a guy down the road got one of them little white floozy dogs, well, she was in heat and the guy locks her up. But my airedale, named Tom he was, he et a woodshed clear down to the roots to get to her. Guy come over one day, he's sore as hell, he says, " I wouldn't mind if my bitch had pups, but Christ Almighty, this morning she slang a litter of Shetland ponies. . . ." (*Takes off hat, scratches his head.*) Got five pups, huh! Gonna keep all of 'em?

SLIM. I don' know, gotta keep 'em awhile, so they can drink Lulu's milk.

CARLSON. (*Thoughtfully.*) Well, looka here, Slim, I been thinkin'. That dog of Candy's is so goddamn old he can't hardly walk. Stinks like hell. Every time Candy brings him in the bunkhouse, I can smell him two or three days. Why don't you get Candy to shoot his ol' dog, and give him one of them pups to raise up? I can smell that dog a mile off. Got no teeth. Can't eat. Candy feeds him milk. He can't chew nothing else. And leadin' him around on a string so he don't bump into things . . . (*The triangle outside begins to ring wildly. Continues for a few moments, then*

29

stops suddenly.) There she goes! (*Outside a burst of voices as men go by.*)

SLIM. (*To* LENNIE *and* GEORGE.) You guys better come on while they's still somethin' to eat. Won't be nothing left in a couple of minutes. (*Exit* SLIM *and* CARLSON. LENNIE *watches* GEORGE *excitedly.*)

LENNIE. George!

GEORGE. (*Rumpling cards into a pile.*) Yeah, I heard 'im, Lennie . . . I'll ask 'im!

LENNIE. (*Excitedly.*) A brown and white one.

GEORGE. Come on, let's get dinner. I don't know whether he's got a brown and white one.

LENNIE. You ask him right away, George, so he won't kill no more of 'em!

GEORGE. Sure! Come on now—let's go. (*They start for door.*)

CURLEY. (*Bounces in, angrily.*) You seen a girl around here?

GEORGE. (*Coldly.*) 'Bout half an hour ago, mebbe.

CURLEY. Well, what the hell was she doin'?

GEORGE. (*Insultingly.*) She said she was lookin' for you.

CURLEY. (*Measures both men with his eyes for a moment.*) Which way did she go?

GEORGE. I don't know. I didn't watch her go. (CURLEY *scowls at him a moment, then turns and hurries out door.*) You know, Lennie, I'm scared I'm gonna tangle with that bastard myself. I hate his guts! Jesus Christ, come on! They won't be a damn thing left to eat.

LENNIE. Will you ask him about a brown and white one? (*They go out.*)

CURTAIN

ACT II

Scene 1

About seven-thirty Friday evening. Same as last scene. The evening light is seen coming in through window, but it is quite dark in bunkhouse. From outside the sounds of a horseshoe game. Thuds on the dirt and occasional clangs as a shoe hits the peg. Now and then voices raised in approval or derision: " That's a good one." . . . " Goddamn right it's a good one." . . . " Here goes for a ringer. I need a ringer." . . . " Goddamn near got it, too."

SLIM and GEORGE come into bunkhouse together. SLIM reaches up and turns on the tin-shaded electric light. Sits down on box at table. GEORGE sits opposite.

SLIM. It wasn't nothing. I would of had to drown most of them pups anyway. No need to thank me about that.

GEORGE. Wasn't much to you, mebbe, but it was a hell of a lot to him. Jesus Christ, I don't know how we're gonna get him to sleep in here. He'll want to stay right out in the barn. We gonna have trouble keepin' him from gettin' right in the box with them pups.

SLIM. Say, you sure was right about him. Maybe he ain't bright —but I never seen such a worker. He damn near killed his partner buckin' barley. He'd take his end of that sack—(*A gesture.*) pretty near kill his partner. God Almighty, I never seen such a strong guy.

GEORGE. (*Proudly.*) You just tell Lennie what to do and he'll do it if it don't take no figuring. (*Outside the sound of horseshoe game goes on: " Son of a bitch if I can win a goddamn game." . . . " Me neither. You'd think them shoes was anvils.")*

SLIM. Funny how you and him string along together.

GEORGE. What's so funny about it?

SLIM. Oh, I don't know. Hardly none of the guys ever travels around together. I hardly never seen two guys travel together.

31

You know how the hands are. They come in and get their bunk and work a month and then they quit and go on alone. Never seem to give a damn about nobody. Jest seems kinda funny. A cuckoo like him and a smart guy like you traveling together.

GEORGE. I ain't so bright neither or I wouldn't be buckin' barley for my fifty and found. If I was bright, if I was even a little bit smart, I'd have my own place and I'd be bringin' in my own crops 'stead of doin' all the work and not gettin' what comes up out of the ground. (*Falls silent for a moment.*)

SLIM. A guy'd like to do that. Sometime I'd like to cuss a string of mules that was my own mules.

GEORGE. It ain't so funny, him and me goin' round together. Him and me was both born in Auburn. I knowed his aunt. She took him when he was a baby and raised him up. When his aunt died Lennie jus' come along with me, out workin'. Got kinda used to each other after a little while.

SLIM. Uh huh.

GEORGE. First I used to have a hell of a lot of fun with him. Used to play jokes on him because he was too dumb to take care of himself. But, hell, he was too dumb even to know when he had a joke played on him. (*Sarcastically.*) Hell, yes, I had fun! Made me seem goddamn smart alongside of him.

SLIM. I seen it that way.

GEORGE. Why, he'd do any damn thing I tole him. If I tole him to walk over a cliff, over he'd go. You know that wasn't so damn much fun after a while. He never got mad about it, neither. I've beat hell out of him and he could bust every bone in my body jest with his hands. But he never lifted a finger against me.

SLIM. (*Braiding a bull whip.*) Even if you socked him, wouldn't he?

GEORGE. No, by God! I tell you what made me stop playing jokes. One day a bunch of guys was standin' aroun' up on the Sacramento River. I was feelin' pretty smart. I turns to Lennie and I says, " Jump in."

SLIM. What happened?

GEORGE. He jumps. Couldn't swim a stroke. He damn near drowned And he was so nice to me for pullin' him out. Clean forgot I tole him to jump in. Well, I ain't done nothin' like that no more. Makes me kinda sick tellin' about it.

SLIM. He's a nice fella. A guy don't need no sense to be a nice fella. Seems to be sometimes it's jest the other way round. Take a real smart guy, he ain't hardly ever a nice fella.

GEORGE. (*Stacking scattered cards, getting solitaire game ready again.*) I ain't got no people. I seen guys that go round on the ranches alone. That ain't no good. They don't have no fun. After a while they get mean.

SLIM. (*Quietly.*) Yeah, I seen 'em get mean. I seen 'em get so they don't want to talk to nobody. Some ways they got to. You take a bunch of guys all livin' in one room an' by God they got to mind their own business. 'Bout the only private thing a guy's got is where he come from and where he's goin'.

GEORGE. 'Course Lennie's a goddamn nuisance most of the time. But you get used to goin' round with a guy and you can't get rid of him. I mean you get used to him an' you can't get rid of bein' used to him. I'm sure drippin' at the mouth. I ain't told nobody all this before.

SLIM. Do you want to git rid of him?

GEORGE. Well, he gets in trouble all the time. Because he's so goddamn dumb. Like what happened in Weed. (*Stops, alarmed at what he has said.*) You wouldn't tell nobody?

SLIM. (*Calmly.*) What did he do in Weed?

GEORGE. You wouldn't tell?—No, course you wouldn't.

SLIM. What did he do?

GEORGE. Well, he seen this girl in a red dress. Dumb bastard like he is he wants to touch everything he likes. Jest wants to feel of it. So he reaches out to feel this red dress. Girl lets out a squawk and that gets Lennie all mixed up. He holds on 'cause that's the only thing he can think to do.

SLIM. The hell!

GEORGE. Well, this girl squawks her head off. I'm right close and I hear all the yellin', so I comes a-running. By that time Lennie's scared to death. You know, I had to sock him over the head with a fence picket to make him let go.

SLIM. So what happens then?

GEORGE. (*Carefully building his solitaire hand.*) Well, she runs in and tells the law she's been raped. The guys in Weed start out to lynch Lennie. So there we sit in an irrigation ditch, under water all the rest of that day. Got only our heads sticking out of water, up under the grass that grows out of the side of the ditch. That night we run outa there.

SLIM. Didn't hurt the girl none, huh?

GEORGE. Hell, no, he jes' scared her.

SLIM. He's a funny guy.

GEORGE. Funny! Why, one time, you know what that big baby done! He was walking along a road —— (*Enter* LENNIE *through* C. *door. Wears coat over his shoulder like a cape and walks hunched over.*) Hi, Lennie. How do you like your pup?

LENNIE. (*Breathlessly.*) He's brown and white jus' like I wanted. (*Goes directly to his bunk and lies down, face to wall, knees drawn up.*)

GEORGE. (*Puts down cards deliberately.*) Lennie!

LENNIE. (*Over his shoulder.*) Huh? What you want, George?

GEORGE. (*Sternly.*) I tole ya, ya couldn't bring that pup in here.

LENNIE. What pup, George? I ain't got no pup. (GEORGE *goes quickly over to him, grabs him by shoulder and rolls him over. Picks up a tiny puppy* [1] *from where* LENNIE *has been concealing it against his stomach.* LENNIE, *quickly.*) Give him to me, George.

GEORGE. You get right up and take this pup to the nest. He's got to sleep with his mother. Ya want ta kill him? Jes' born last night and ya take him out of the nest. Ya take him back or I'll tell Slim not to let you have him.

LENNIE. (*Pleadingly.*) Give him to me, George. I'll take him back. I didn't mean no bad thing, George. Honest I didn't. I jus' want to pet him a little.

GEORGE. (*Giving pup to him.*) All right, you get him back there quick. And don't you take him out no more. (LENNIE *scuttles out of room.*)

SLIM. Jesus, he's just like a kid, ain't he?

GEORGE. Sure he's like a kid. There ain't no more harm in him than a kid neither, except he's so strong. I bet he won't come in here to sleep tonight. He'll sleep right alongside that box in the barn. Well, let him. He ain't doin' no harm out there. (*Light has faded outside and it appears quite dark there. Enter* CANDY *leading his old dog by a string.*)

CANDY. Hello, Slim. Hello, George. Don't neither of you play horseshoes?

SLIM. I don't like to play every night.

CANDY. (*Goes to his bunk, sits down, presses dog to floor beside him.*) Either you guys got a slug of whiskey? I got a gut ache.

[1] Can be a dummy or roll of cloth.

34

SLIM. I ain't. I'd drink it myself if I had. And I ain't got no gut ache either.

CANDY. Goddamn cabbage give it to me. I knowed it was goin' to before I ever et it. (*Enter* CARLSON *and* WHIT.)

CARLSON. Jesus, how that nigger can pitch shoes!

SLIM. He's plenty good.

WHIT. Damn right he is.

CARLSON. Yeah. He don't give nobody else a chance to win. (*Stops and sniffs the air. Looks around until he sees* CANDY'S *dog.*) God Almighty, that dog stinks. Get him outa here, Candy. I don't know nothing that stinks as bad as ole dogs. You got to get him outa here.

CANDY. (*Lying on his bunk, reaches over, pats dog, speaks softly.*) I been round him so much I never notice how he stinks.

CARLSON. Well, I can't stand him in here. That stink hangs round even after he's gone. (*Walks over, stands looking down at dog.*) Got no teeth. All stiff with rheumatism. He ain't no good to you, Candy. Why don't you shoot him?

CANDY. (*Uncomfortably.*) Well, hell, I had him so long! Had him since he was a pup. I herded sheep with him. (*Proudly.*) You wouldn't think it to look at him now. He was the best damn sheep dog I ever seen.

GEORGE. I knowed a guy in Weed that had an airedale that could herd sheep. Learned it from the other dogs.

CARLSON. (*Sticking to his point.*) Lookit, Candy. This ole dog jus' suffers itself all the time. If you was to take him out and shoot him—right in back of the head . . . (*Leans over and points.*) . . . right there, why he never'd know what hit him.

CANDY. (*Unhappily.*) No, I couldn't do that. I had him too long.

CARLSON. (*Insisting.*) He don't have no fun no more. He stinks like hell. Tell you what I'll do. I'll shoot him for you. Then it won't be you that done it.

CANDY. (*Sits up on bunk, rubbing whiskers nervously, speaks plaintively.*) I had him from a pup.

WHIT. Let 'im alone, Carl. It ain't a guy's dog that matters. It's the way the guy feels about the dog. Hell, I had a mutt once I wouldn't a traded for a field trial pointer.

CARLSON. (*Being persuasive.*) Well, Candy ain't being nice to him, keeping him alive. Lookit, Slim's bitch got a litter right now. I bet you Slim would give ya one of them pups to raise up, wouldn't ya, Slim?

SLIM. (*Studying dog.*) Yeah. You can have a pup if you want to.

CANDY. (*Helplessly.*) Mebbe it would hurt. (*After a moment's pause, positively.*) And I don't mind taking care of him.

CARLSON. Aw, he'd be better off dead. The way I'd shoot him he wouldn't feel nothin'. I'd put the gun right there. (*Points with his toe.*) Right back of the head.

WHIT. Aw, let 'im alone, Carl.

CARLSON. Why, hell, he wouldn't even quiver.

WHIT. Let 'im alone. (*Produces magazine.*) Say, did you see this? Did you see this in the book here?

CARLSON. See what?

WHIT. Right there. Read that.

CARLSON. I don't want to read nothing. . . . It'd be all over in a minute, Candy. Come on.

WHIT. Did you see it, Slim? Go on, read it. Read it out loud.

SLIM. What is it?

WHIT. Read it.

SLIM. (*Reads slowly.*) "Dear Editor: I read your mag for six years and I think it is the best on the market. I like stories by Peter Rand. I think he is a whing-ding. Give us more like the Dark Rider. I don't write many letters. Just thought I would tell you I think your mag is the best dime's worth I ever spen'." (*Looks up questioningly.*) What you want me to read that for?

WHIT. Go on, read the name at the bottom.

SLIM. (*Reading.*) "Yours for Success, William Tenner." (*Looks up at* WHIT.) What ya want me to read that for?

CARLSON. Come on, Candy—what you say?

WHIT. (*Taking magazine, closing it impressively. Talks to cover* CARLSON.) You don't remember Bill Tenner? Worked here about three months ago?

SLIM. (*Thinking.*) Little guy? Drove a cultivator?

WHIT. That's him. That's the guy.

CARLSON. (*Has refused to be drawn into conversation.*) Look, Candy. If you want me to, I'll put the old devil outa his misery right now and get it over with. There ain't nothin' left for him. Can't eat, can't see, can't hardly walk. Tomorrow you can pick one of Slim's pups.

SLIM. Sure . . . I got a lot of 'em.

CANDY. (*Hopefully.*) You ain't got no gun.

CARLSON. The hell I ain't. Got a Luger. It won't hurt him none at all.

CANDY. Mebbe tomorrow. Let's wait till tomorrow.

CARLSON. I don't see no reason for it. (*Goes to his bunk, pulls bag from underneath, takes revolver out.*) Let's get it over with. We can't sleep with him stinking around in here. (*Snaps shell into chamber, sets safety, puts revolver into hip pocket.*)

SLIM. (*As* CANDY *looks toward him for help.*) Better let him go, Candy.

CANDY. (*Looks at each person for some hope.* WHIT *makes gesture of protest, then resigns himself. Others look away, to avoid responsibility. At last, very softly and hopelessly.*) All right. Take him. (*He doesn't look down at dog at all. Lies back on his bunk, crosses his arms behind his head, stares at ceiling.* CARLSON *picks up string, helps dog to its feet.*)

CARLSON. Come, boy. Come on, boy. (*To* CANDY, *apologetically.*) He won't even feel it. (CANDY *does not move nor answer.*) Come on, boy. That's the stuff. Come on. (*Leads dog toward door.*)

SLIM. Carlson?

CARLSON. Yeah.

SLIM. (*Curtly.*) Take a shovel.

CARLSON. Oh, sure, I get you. (*Exit* CARLSON *with dog.* GEORGE *follows to door, shuts it carefully, sets latch.* CANDY *lies rigidly on his bunk. Next scene is one of silence and quick staccato speeches.*)

SLIM. (*Loudly.*) One of my lead mules got a bad hoof. Got to get some tar on it. (*A silence.*)

GEORGE. (*Loudly.*) Anybody like to play a little euchre?

WHIT. I'll lay out a few with you. (*They take places opposite each other at table but* GEORGE *does not shuffle cards. Ripples edge of deck. Everybody looks over at him. He stops. Silence again.*)

SLIM. (*Compassionately.*) Candy, you can have any of them pups you want. (*No answer from* CANDY. *There is a little gnawing noise on stage.*)

GEORGE. Sounds like there was a rat under there. We ought to set a trap there. (*Deep silence again.*)

WHIT. (*Exasperated.*) What the hell is takin' him so long? Lay out some cards, why don't you? We ain't gonna get no euchre played this way. (GEORGE *studies backs of cards. After long si-*

lence, a shot in the distance. All start a bit, look quickly at CANDY. *For a moment he continues to stare at ceiling, then rolls slowly over and faces wall.* GEORGE *shuffles cards noisily, deals them.)*

GEORGE. Well, let's get to it.

WHIT. (*Still to cover the moment.*) Yeah . . . I guess you guys really come here to work, huh?

GEORGE. How do you mean?

WHIT. (*Chuckles.*) Well, you come on a Friday. You got two days to work till Sunday.

GEORGE. I don't see how you figure.

WHIT. You do if you been round these big ranches much. A guy that wants to look over a ranch comes in Saturday afternoon. He gets Saturday night supper, three meals on Sunday and he can quit on Monday morning after breakfast without turning a hand. But you come to work on Friday noon. You got ta put in a day and a half no matter how ya figure it.

GEORGE. (*Quietly.*) We're goin' stick around awhile. Me and Lennie's gonna roll up a stake. (*Door opens.* CROOKS *puts in his head: lean-faced Negro with pained eyes.*)

CROOKS. Mr. Slim.

SLIM. (*Who has been watching* CANDY.) Huh? Oh, hello, Crooks, what's the matter?

CROOKS. You tole me to warm up tar for that mule's foot. I got it warm now.

SLIM. Oh, sure, Crooks. I'll come right out and put it on.

CROOKS. I can do it for you if you want, Mr. Slim.

SLIM. (*Standing up.*) Naw, I'll take care of my own team.

CROOKS. Mr. Slim.

SLIM. Yeah.

CROOKS. That big new guy is messing round your pups in the barn.

SLIM. Well, he ain't doin' no harm. I give him one of them pups.

CROOKS. Just thought I'd tell ya. He's takin' 'em out of the nest and handling 'em. That won't do 'em no good.

SLIM. Oh, he won't hurt 'em.

GEORGE. (*Looks up from cards.*) If that crazy bastard is foolin' round too much jus' kick him out. (SLIM *follows* CROOKS *out.*)

WHIT. (*Examining cards.*) Seen the new kid yet?

GEORGE. What kid?

WHIT. Why, Curley's new wife.

GEORGE. (*Cautiously.*) Yeah, I seen her.

WHIT. Well, ain't she a lulu?

GEORGE. I ain't seen that much of her.

WHIT. Well, you stick around and keep your eyes open. You'll see plenty of her. I never seen nobody like her. She's just workin' on everybody all the time. Seems like she's even workin' on the stable buck. I don't know what the hell she wants.

GEORGE. (*Casually.*) Been any trouble since she got here? (*Obviously neither is interested in game.* WHIT *lays down his hand,* GEORGE *gathers cards in, lays out solitaire hand.*)

WHIT. I see what you mean. No, they ain't been no trouble yet. She's only been here a couple of weeks. Curley's got yellow jackets in his drawers, but that's all so far. Every time the guys is around she shows up. She's lookin' for Curley. Or she thought she left somethin' layin' around and she's lookin' for that. Seems like she can't keep away from guys. And Curley's runnin' round like a cat lookin' for a dirt road. But they ain't been no trouble.

GEORGE. Ranch with a bunch of guys on it ain't no place for a girl. Specially like her.

WHIT. If she's give you any ideas you ought to come in town with us guys tomorrow night.

GEORGE. Why, what's doin'?

WHIT. Just the usual thing. We go in to old Susy's place. Hell of a nice place. Old Susy is a laugh. Always cracking jokes. Like she says when we come up on the front porch last Saturday night: Susy opens the door and she yells over her shoulder: " Get your coats on, girls, here comes the sheriff." She never talks dirty neither. Got five girls there.

GEORGE. What does it set you back?

WHIT. Two and a half. You can get a shot of whiskey for fifteen cents. Susy got nice chairs to set in too. If a guy don't want to flop, why, he can just set in them chairs and have a couple or three shots and just pass the time of day. Susy don't give a damn. She ain't rushin' guys through, or kicking them out if they don't want to flop.

GEORGE. Might go in and look the joint over.

WHIT. Sure. Come along. It's a hell of a lot of fun—her crackin' jokes all the time. Like she says one time, she says. " I've knew people that if they got a rag rug on the floor and a kewpie doll lamp on the phonograph they think they're runnin' a parlor house." That's Gladys's house she's talkin' about. And Susy says:

"I know what you boys want," she says: "My girls is clean," she says. "And there ain't no water in my whiskey," she says. "If any you guys want to look at a kewpie doll lamp and take your chance of gettin' burned, why, you know where to go." She says: "They's guys round here walkin' bowlegged because they liked to look at a kewpie doll lamp."

GEORGE. Gladys runs the other house, huh?

WHIT. Yeah. (*Enter* CARLSON. CANDY *looks at him.*)

CARLSON. God, it's a dark night. (*Goes to his bunk, starts cleaning his revolver.*)

WHIT. We don't never go to Gladys's. Gladys gits three bucks, and two bits a shot and she don't crack no jokes. But Susy's place is clean and she got nice chairs. A guy can set in there like he lived there. Don't let no Manila Goo-Goos in, neither.

GEORGE. Aw, I don't know. Me and Lennie's rollin' up a stake. I might go in and set and have a shot, but I ain't puttin' out no two and a half.

WHIT. Well, a guy got to have some fun sometimes. (*Enter* LENNIE, *who creeps to his bunk, sits down.*)

GEORGE. Didn't bring him back in, did you, Lennie?

LENNIE. No, George, honest I didn't. See?

WHIT. Say, how about this euchre game?

GEORGE. Okay. I didn't think you wanted to play. (*Enter* CURLEY *excitedly.*)

CURLEY. Any you guys seen my wife?

WHIT. She ain't been here.

CURLEY. (*Looks threateningly about.*) Where the hell's Slim?

GEORGE. Went out in the barn. He was goin' put some tar on a split hoof.

CURLEY. How long ago did he go?

GEORGE. Oh, five, ten minutes. (CURLEY *jumps out the door.*)

WHIT. (*Standing up.*) I guess maybe I'd like to see this. Curley must be spoilin' or he wouldn't start for Slim. Curley's handy, goddamn handy. But just the same he better leave Slim alone.

GEORGE. Thinks Slim's with his wife, don't he?

WHIT. Looks like it. 'Course Slim ain't. Least I don't think Slim is. But I like to see the fuss if it comes off. Come on, le's go.

GEORGE. I don't want to git mixed up in nothing. Me and Lennie got to make a stake.

CARLSON. (*Finishes cleaning revolver, puts it in his bag, stands up.*)

I'll look her over. Ain't seen a good fight in a hell of a while. (WHIT *and* CARLSON *go out.*)

GEORGE. You see Slim out in the barn?

LENNIE. Sure. He tole me I better not pet that pup no more, like I said.

GEORGE. Did you see that girl out there?

LENNIE. You mean Curley's girl?

GEORGE. Yeah. Did she come in the barn?

LENNIE. (*Cautiously.*) No—anyways I never seen her.

GEORGE. You never seen Slim talkin' to her?

LENNIE. Uh-uh. She ain't been in the barn.

GEORGE. Okay. I guess them guys ain't gonna see no fight. If they's any fightin', Lennie, ya get out of the way and stay out.

LENNIE. I don't want no fight. (GEORGE *lays out solitaire hand.* LENNIE *picks up face card, studies it. Turns it over, studies it again.*) Both ends the same. George, why is it both ends the same?

GEORGE. I don't know. That jus' the way they make 'em. What was Slim doin' in the barn when you seen him?

LENNIE. Slim?

GEORGE. Sure, you seen him in the barn. He tole you not to pet the pups so much.

LENNIE. Oh. Yeah. He had a can of tar and a paint brush. I don't know what for.

GEORGE. You sure that girl didn't come in like she come in here today?

LENNIE. No, she never come.

GEORGE. (*Sighs.*) You give me a good cat-house every time. A guy can go in and get drunk and get it over all at once and no messes. And he knows how much it's goin' set him back. These tarts is jus' buckshot to a guy. (LENNIE *listens with admiration, moving his lips.* GEORGE *continues.*) You remember Andy Cushman, Lennie? Went to grammar school same time as us?

LENNIE. The one that his ole lady used to make hot cakes for the kids?

GEORGE. Yeah. That's the one. You can remember if they's somepin to eat in it. (*Scores cards in his solitaire playing.*) Well, Andy's in San Quentin right now on account of a tart.

LENNIE. George?

GEORGE. Huh?

41

LENNIE. How long is it goin' be till we git that little place to live on the fat of the land?

GEORGE. I don't know. We gotta get a big stake together. I know a little place we can get cheap, but they ain't givin' it away. (CANDY *turns slowly over, watches* GEORGE.)

LENNIE. Tell about that place, George.

GEORGE. I jus' tole you. Jus' last night.

LENNIE. Go on, tell again.

GEORGE. Well, it's ten acres. Got a little windmill. Got a little shack on it and a chicken run. Got a kitchen orchard. Cherries, apples, peaches, 'cots and nuts. Got a few berries. There's a place for alfalfa and plenty water to flood it. There's a pig pen . . .

LENNIE. (*Breaking in.*) And rabbits, George?

GEORGE. I could easy build a few hutches. And you could feed alfalfa to them rabbits.

LENNIE. Damn right I could. (*Excitedly.*) You goddamn right I could.

GEORGE. (*His voice growing warmer.*) And we could have a few pigs. I'd build a smokehouse. And when we kill a pig we could smoke the hams. When the salmon run up the river we can catch a hundred of 'em. Every Sunday we'd kill a chicken or rabbit. Mebbe we'll have a cow or a goat. And the cream is so goddamn thick you got to cut it off the pan with a knife.

LENNIE. (*Watching him with wide eyes, softly.*) We can live off the fat of the land.

GEORGE. Sure. All kinds of vegetables in the garden and if we want a little whiskey we can sell some eggs or somethin'. And we wouldn't sleep in no bunkhouse. Nobody could can us in the middle of a job.

LENNIE. (*Begging.*) Tell about the house, George.

GEORGE. Sure. We'd have a little house. And a room to ourselves. And it ain't enough land so we'd have to work too hard. Mebbe six, seven hours a day only. We wouldn't have to buck no barley eleven hours a day. And when we put in a crop, why we'd be there to take that crop up. We'd know what come of our planting.

LENNIE. (*Eagerly.*) And rabbits. And I'd take care of them. Tell how I'd do that, George.

GEORGE. Sure. You'd go out in the alfalfa patch and you'd have a sack. You'd fill up the sack and bring it in and put it in the rabbit cages.

LENNIE. They'd nibble and they'd nibble, the way they do. I seen 'em.

GEORGE. Every six weeks or so them does would throw a litter. So we'd have plenty rabbits to eat or sell. (*Pauses for inspiration.*) And we'd keep a few pigeons to go flying round and round the windmill, like they done when I was a kid. (*Seems entranced.*) And it'd be our own. And nobody could can us. If we don't like a guy we can say: " Get to hell out," and by God he's got to do it. And if a friend come along, why, we'd have an extra bunk. Know what we'd say? We'd say, " Why don't you spen' the night? " And by God he would. We'd have a setter dog and a couple of striped cats. (*Looks sharply at* LENNIE.) But you gotta watch out them cats don't get the little rabbits.

LENNIE. (*Breathing hard.*) You jus' let 'em try. I'll break their goddamn necks. I'll smash them cats flat with a stick. I'd smash 'em flat with a stick. That's what I'd do. (*They sit silently for a moment.*)

CANDY. (*At sound of his voice, both* LENNIE *and* GEORGE *jump as though caught in some secret.*) You know where's a place like that?

GEORGE. (*Solemnly.*) S'pose I do, what's that to you?

CANDY. You don't need to tell me where it's at. Might be any place.

GEORGE. (*Relieved.*) Sure. That's right, you couldn't find it in a hundred years.

CANDY. (*Excitedly.*) How much they want for a place like that?

GEORGE. (*Grudgingly.*) Well, I could get it for six hundred bucks. The ole people that owns it is flat bust. And the ole lady needs medicine. Say, what's it to you? You got nothing to do with us!

CANDY. (*Softly.*) I ain't much good with only one hand. I lost my hand right here on the ranch. That's why they didn't can me. They give me a job swampin'. And they give me two hundred and fifty dollars 'cause I lost my hand. An' I got fifty more saved up right in the bank right now. That's three hundred. And I got forty more comin' the end of the month. Tell you what . . . (*Leans forward eagerly.*) S'pose I went in with you guys? That's three hundred and forty bucks I'd put in. I ain't much good, but I could cook and tend the chickens and hoe the garden some. How'd that be?

GEORGE. (*Eyes half closed, uncertainly.*) I got to think about that.

43

We was always goin' to do it by ourselves. Me an' Lennie. I never thought of nobody else.

CANDY. I'd make a will. Leave my share to you guys in case I kicked off. I ain't got no relations nor nothing. You fellas got any money? Maybe we could go there right now.

GEORGE. (*Disgustedly.*) We got ten bucks between us. (*He thinks.*) Say, look. If me and Lennie work a month and don't spend nothing at all, we'll have a hundred bucks. That would be four-forty. I bet we could swing her for that. Then you and Lennie could go get her started and I'd get a job and make up the rest. You could sell eggs and stuff like that. (*They look at each other in amazement. Reverently.*) Jesus Christ, I bet we could swing her. (*His voice is full of wonder.*) I bet we could swing 'er.

CANDY. (*Scratches stump of his wrist nervously.*) I got hurt four years ago. They'll can me pretty soon. Jest as soon as I can't swamp out no bunkhouses they'll put me on the county. Maybe if I give you guys my money, you'll let me hoe in the garden, even when I ain't no good at it. And I'll wash dishes and little chicken stuff like that. But hell, I'll be on our own place. I'll be let to work on our own place. (*Miserably.*) You seen what they done to my dog. They says he wasn't no good to himself nor nobody else. But when I'm that way nobody'll shoot me. I wish somebody would. They won't do nothing like that. I won't have no place to go and I can't get no more jobs.

GEORGE. (*Stands up.*) We'll do 'er! God damn, we'll fix up that little ole place and we'll go live there. (*Wonderingly.*) S'pose they was a carnival, or a circus come to town or a ball game or any damn thing. (CANDY *nods in appreciation.*) We'd just go to her. We wouldn't ask nobody if we could. Just say we'll go to her, by God, and we would. Just milk the cow and sling some grain to the chickens and go to her.

LENNIE. And put some grass to the rabbits. I wouldn't forget to feed them. When we gonna to do it, George?

GEORGE. (*Decisively.*) In one month. Right smack in one month. Know what I'm gonna do? I'm goin' write to them ole people that owns the place that we'll take 'er. And Candy'll send a hundred dollars to bind her.

CANDY. (*Happily.*) I sure will. They got a good stove there?

GEORGE. Sure, got a nice stove. Burns coal or wood.

LENNIE. I'm gonna take my pup. I bet by Christ he likes it there.

(*Window* U. C. *swings outward.* CURLEY'S WIFE *looks in. They do not see her.*)

GEORGE. (*Quickly.*) Now don't tell nobody about her. Jus' us three and nobody else. They're liable to can us so we can't make no stake. We'll just go on like we was a bunch of punks. Like we was gonna buck barley the rest of our lives. And then all of a sudden, one day, bang! We get our pay and scram out of here.

CANDY. I can give you three hundred right now.

LENNIE. And not tell nobody. We won't tell nobody, George.

GEORGE. You're goddamn right we won't. (*A silence, then* GEORGE *speaks irritably.*) You know, seems to me I can almost smell that carnation stuff that goddamn tart dumps on herself.

CURLEY'S WIFE. (*In first part of* GEORGE'S *speech she starts to step out of sight, but at last words her face darkens with anger. At her first words everybody looks around at her and remains rigid.*) Who you callin' a tart! I come from a nice home. I was brung up by nice people. Nobody never got to me before I was married. I was straight. I tell you I was good. (*A little plaintively.*) I was. (*Angrily again.*) You know Curley. You know he wouldn't stay with me if he wasn't sure. I tell you Curley is sure. You got no right to call me a tart.

GEORGE. (*Sullenly.*) If you ain't a tart, what you always hangin' round guys for? You got a house an' you got a man. We don't want no trouble from you.

CURLEY'S WIFE. (*Pleadingly.*) Sure I got a man. He ain't never home. I got nobody to talk to. I got nobody to be with. Think I can just sit home and do nothin' but cook for Curley? I want to see somebody. Just see 'em an' talk to 'em. There ain't no women. I can't walk to town. And Curley don't take me to no dances now. I tell you I jus' want to talk to somebody.

GEORGE. (*Boldly.*) If you're just friendly what you givin' out the eye for an' floppin' your can around?

CURLEY'S WIFE. (*Sadly.*) I just wanta be nice. (*Sound of approaching voices:* "*You don't have to get mad about it, do you?*" . . . "*I ain't mad, but I just don't want no more questions, that's all. I just don't want no more questions.*")

GEORGE. Get goin'. We don't want no trouble. (CURLEY'S WIFE *looks from window, closes it silently, disappears. Enter* SLIM, *followed by* CURLEY, CARLSON *and* WHIT. SLIM'S *hands are black with tar.* CURLEY *hangs close to his elbow.*)

CURLEY. (*Explaining.*) Well, I didn't mean nothing, Slim. I jus' ast you.

SLIM. Well, you been askin' too often. I'm gettin' goddamn sick of it. If you can't look after your own wife, what you expect me to do about it? You lay off of me.

CURLEY. I'm jus' tryin' to tell you I didn't mean nothing. I just thought you might of saw her.

CARLSON. Why don't you tell her to stay to hell home where she belongs? You let her hang around the bunkhouses and pretty soon you're goin' have somethin' on your hands.

CURLEY. (*Whirls on* CARLSON.) You keep out of this 'less you want ta step outside.

CARLSON. (*Laughing.*) Why, you goddamn punk. You tried to throw a scare into Slim and you couldn't make it stick. Slim throwed a scare into you. You're yellow as a frog's belly. I don't care if you're the best boxer in the country, you come for me and I'll kick your goddamn head off.

WHIT. (*Joining in the attack.*) Glove full of vaseline!

CURLEY. (*Glares at him, then suddenly sniffs the air, like a hound.*) By God, she's been in here. I can smell —— By God, she's been in here. (*To* GEORGE.) You was here. The other guys was outside. Now, God damn you—you talk.

GEORGE. (*Looks worried. Seems to make up his mind to face an inevitable situation. Stands. Slowly takes off his coat, folds it almost daintily. Speaks in an unemotional monotone.*) Somebody got to beat the hell outa you. I guess I'm elected. (LENNIE *has been watching, fascinated. Gives his high, nervous chuckle.*)

CURLEY. (*Whirls on him.*) What the hell you laughin' at?

LENNIE. (*Blankly.*) Huh?

CURLEY. (*Exploding with rage.*) Come on; you big bastard. Get up on your feet. No big son-of-a-bitch is gonna laugh at me. I'll show you who's yellow. (LENNIE *looks helplessly at* GEORGE. *Gets up, tries to retreat upstage.* CURLEY *follows, slashing at him. Others mass themselves in front of the contestants:* " *That ain't no way, Curly—he ain't done nothing to you.*" . . . " *Lay off him, will you, Curly. He ain't no fighter.*" . . . " *Sock him back, big guy! Don't be afraid of him!* " . . . " *Give him a chance, Curly. Give him a chance.*")

LENNIE. (*Crying with terror.*) George, make him leave me alone, George.

46

GEORGE. Get him, Lennie. Get him! (*A sharp cry. The gathering of men opens and* CURLEY *is flopping about, his hand lost in* LENNIE'S *hand.*) Let go of him, Lennie. Let go! ("*He's got his hand!*" . . , "*Look at that, will you?*" . . . "*Jesus, what a guy!*" LENNIE *watches in terror the flopping man he holds.* LENNIE'S *face is covered with blood.* GEORGE *slaps* LENNIE *in the face again and again.* CURLEY *is weak and shrunken.*) Let go his hand, Lennie. Slim, come help me, while this guy's got any hand left. (*Suddenly* LENNIE *lets go. Cowers away from* GEORGE.)

LENNIE. You told me to, George. I heard you tell me to. (CURLEY *has dropped to floor.* SLIM *and* CARLSON *bend over him and look at his hand.* SLIM *looks at* LENNIE *with horror.*

SLIM. We got to get him to a doctor. It looks to me like every bone in his hand is busted.

LENNIE. (*Crying.*) I didn't wanta. I didn't wanta hurt 'im.

SLIM. Carlson, you get the candy wagon out. He'll have to go into Soledad and get his hand fixed up. (*Turns to the whimpering* LENNIE.) It ain't your fault. This punk had it comin' to him. But Jesus—he ain't hardly got no hand left.

GEORGE. (*Moving near.*) Slim, will we git canned now? Will Curley's ole man can us now?

SLIM. I don't know. (*Kneels beside* CURLEY.) You got your sense enough to listen? (CURLEY *nods.*) Well, then you listen. I think you got your hand caught in a machine. If you don't tell nobody what happened, we won't. But you jest tell and try to get this guy canned and we'll tell everybody. And then will you get the laugh! (*Helps* CURLEY *to his feet.*) Come on now. Carlson's goin' to take you in to a doctor. (*Starts for door, turns back to* LENNIE.) Let's see your hands. (LENNIE *sticks out both hands.*) Christ Almighty!

GEORGE. Lennie was just scairt. He didn't know what to do. I tole you nobody ought never to fight him. No, I guess it was Candy I tole.

CANDY. (*Solemnly.*) That's just what you done. Right this morning when Curley first lit into him. You says he better not fool with Lennie if he knows what's good for him. (*All leave except* GEORGE, LENNIE *and* CANDY.)

GEORGE. (*To* LENNIE, *very gently.*) It ain't your fault. You don't need to be scairt no more. You done jus' what I tole you to.

Maybe you better go in the washroom and clean up your face.
You look like hell.

LENNIE. I didn't want no trouble.

GEORGE. Come on —— I'll go with you.

LENNIE. George?

GEORGE. What you want?

LENNIE. Can I still tend the rabbits, George? (*They go out to-gether, side by side, through door.*)

CURTAIN

ACT II

SCENE 2

Ten o'clock Saturday evening.

The room of the stable buck Crooks, a lean-to off barn. There is a plank door up C.; a small square window R. C. On one side of door a leather working bench with tools racked behind it, and on other, racks with broken and partly mended harnesses, collars, hames, traces, etc. U. L. Crooks' bunk. Over it two shelves. On one a great number of medicine cans and bottles. On the other a number of tattered books and a big alarm clock. U. R. a single-barreled shotgun and on floor beside it a pair of rubber boots. A large pair of gold spectacles hangs on a nail over Crooks' bunk.

Entrance leads into barn proper. From that direction and during the whole scene come the sounds of horses eating, stamping, jingling their halter chains, and now and then whinnying. Two empty nail kegs are in the room to be used as seats. Single unshaded small-candle-power carbon light hanging from its own cord.[1]

As curtain rises, CROOKS sits on his bunk rubbing his back with liniment. Reaches up under his shirt to do this. His face is lined with pain. As he rubs he flexes his muscles and shivers a little. LENNIE appears in open doorway, nearly filling the opening. Then CROOKS, sens-

[1] See p. 5, *Production Note.*

ing his presence, raises his eyes, stiffens and scowls.
LENNIE *smiles in an attempt to make friends.*

CROOKS. (*Sharply.*) You got no right to come in my room. This here's my room. Nobody got any right in here but me.

LENNIE. (*Fawning.*) I ain't doin' nothing. Just come in the barn to look at my pup, and I seen your light.

CROOKS. Well, I got a right to have a light. You go on and get out of my room. I ain't wanted in the bunkhouse and you ain't wanted in my room.

LENNIE. (*Ingenuously.*) Why ain't you wanted?

CROOKS. (*Furiously.*) 'Cause I'm black. They play cards in there. But I can't play because I'm black. They say I stink. Well, I tell you all of you stink to me.

LENNIE. (*Helplessly.*) Everybody went into town. Slim and George and everybody. George says I got to stay here and not get into no trouble. I seen your light.

CROOKS. Well, what do you want?

LENNIE. Nothing . . . I seen your light. I thought I could jus' come in and set.

CROOKS. (*Stares at* LENNIE *a moment, takes down spectacles, adjusts them over his ears, says in a complaining tone.*) I don't know what you're doin' in the barn anyway. You ain't no skinner. There's no call for a bucker to come into the barn at all. You've got nothing to do with the horses and mules.

LENNIE. (*Patiently.*) The pup. I come to see my pup.

CROOKS. Well, God damn it, go and see your pup then. Don't go no place where you ain't wanted.

LENNIE. (*Advances a step into the room, remembers and backs to door again.*) I looked at him a little. Slim says I ain't to pet him very much.

CROOKS. (*Anger gradually going out of his voice.*) Well, you been taking him out of the nest all the time. I wonder the ole lady don't move him some place else.

LENNIE (*Moving into room.*) Oh, she don't care. She lets me.

CROOKS. (*Scowls, then gives up.*) Come on in and set awhile. Long as you won't get out and leave me alone, you might as well set down. (*A little more friendly.*) All the boys gone into town, huh?

LENNIE. All but old Candy. He jus' sets in the bunkhouse sharpening his pencils. And sharpening and figurin'.

CROOKS. (*Adjusting glasses.*) Figurin'? What's Candy figurin' about?

LENNIE. 'Bout the land. 'Bout the little place.

CROOKS. You're nuts. You're crazy as a wedge. What land you talkin' about?

LENNIE. The land we're goin' ta get. And a little house and pigeons.

CROOKS. Just nuts. I don't blame the guy you're traveling with for keeping you out of sight.

LENNIE. (*Quietly.*) It ain't no lie. We're gonna do it. Gonna get a little place and live on the fat of the land.

CROOKS. (*Settling himself comfortably on his bunk.*) Set down. Set down on that nail keg.

LENNIE. (*Hunches over on little barrel.*) You think it's a lie. But it ain't no lie. Ever' word's the truth. You can ask George.

CROOKS. (*Puts chin on his palm.*) You travel round with George, don't you?

LENNIE. (*Proudly.*) Sure, me and him goes ever' place together.

CROOKS. (*After pause, quietly.*) Sometimes he talks and you don't know what the hell he's talkin' about. Ain't that so? (*Leans forward.*) Ain't that so?

LENNIE. Yeah. Sometimes.

CROOKS. Just talks on. And you don't know what the hell it's all about.

LENNIE. How long you think it'll be before them pups will be old enough to pet?

CROOKS. (*Laughs again.*) A guy can talk to you and be sure you won't go blabbin'. A couple of weeks and them pups will be all right. (*Musing.*) George knows what he's about. Just talks and you don't understand nothing. (*Mood gradually changes to excitement.*) Well, this is just a nigger talkin', and a busted-back nigger. It don't mean nothing, see. You couldn't remember it anyway. I seen it over and over—a guy talking to another guy and it don't make no difference if he don't hear or understand. The thing is they're talkin'. (*Pounds knee with his hand.*) George can tell you screwy things and it don't matter. It's just the talkin'. It's just bein' with another guy, that's all. (*His voice becomes soft and malicious.*) S'pose George don't come back no more? S'pose he took a powder and just ain't comin' back. What you do then?

LENNIE. (*Trying to follow* CROOKS.) What? What?

CROOKS. I said s'pose George went into town tonight and you never heard of him no more. (*Presses forward.*) Just s'pose that.
LENNIE. (*Sharply.*) He won't do it. George wouldn't do nothing like that. I been with George a long time. He'll come back to-night. . . . (*Doubt creeps into his voice.*) Don't you think he will?
CROOKS. (*Delighted with his torture.*) Nobody can tell what a guy will do. Let's say he wants to come back and can't. S'pose he gets killed or hurt so he can't come back.
LENNIE. (*In terrible apprehension.*) I don't know. Say, what you doin' anyway? It ain't true. George ain't got hurt.
CROOKS. (*Cruelly.*) Want me to tell you what'll happen? They'll take you to the booby hatch. They'll tie you up with a collar like a dog. Then you'll be jus' like me. Livin' in a kennel.
LENNIE. (*Furious, walks over toward CROOKS.*) Who hurt George?
CROOKS. (*Recoiling with fright.*) I was just supposin'. George ain't hurt. He's all right. He'll be back all right.
LENNIE. (*Standing over him.*) What you supposin' for? Ain't nobody goin' to s'pose any hurt to George.
CROOKS. (*Trying to calm him.*) Now set down. George ain't hurt. Go on now, set down.
LENNIE. (*Growling.*) Ain't nobody gonna talk no hurt to George.
CROOKS. (*Very gently.*) Maybe you can see now. You got George. You know he's comin' back. S'pose you didn't have nobody. S'pose you couldn't go in the bunkhouse and play rummy, 'cause you was black. How would you like that? S'pose you had to set out here and read books. Sure, you could play horseshoes until it got dark, but then you got to read books. Books ain't no good. A guy needs somebody . . . to be near him. (*His tone whines.*) A guy goes nuts if he ain't got nobody. Don't make no difference who it is as long as he's with you. I tell you a guy gets too lonely, he gets sick.
LENNIE. (*Reassuring himself.*) George gonna come back. Maybe George come back already. Maybe I better go see.
CROOKS. (*More gently.*) I didn't mean to scare you. He'll come back. I was talkin' about myself.
LENNIE. (*Miserably.*) George won't go away and leave me. I know George won't do that.
CROOKS. (*Continuing dreamily.*) I remember when I was a little kid on my ole man's chicken ranch. Had two brothers. They was

51

always near me, always there. Used to sleep right in the same room. Right in the same bed, all three. Had a strawberry patch. Had an alfalfa patch. Used to turn the chickens out in the alfalfa patch on a sunny morning. Me and my brothers would set on the fence and watch 'em—white chickens they was.

LENNIE. (*Interested.*) George says we're gonna have alfalfa.

CROOKS. You're nuts.

LENNIE. We are too gonna get it. You ask George.

CROOKS. (*Scornfully.*) You're nuts. I seen hundreds of men come by on the road and on the ranches, bindles on their back and that same damn thing in their head. Hundreds of 'em. They come and they quit and they go on. And every damn one of 'em is got a little piece of land in his head. And never a goddamn one of 'em gets it. Jus' like heaven. Everybody wants a little piece of land. Nobody never gets to heaven. And nobody gets no land.

LENNIE. We are too.

CROOKS. It's jest in your head. Guys all the time talkin' about it, but it's jest in your head. (*Horses move restlessly off stage. One of them whinnies.*) I guess somebody's out there. Maybe Slim. (*Pulls himself painfully upright, moves toward door. Calls.*) That you, Slim?

CANDY. (*From outside.*) Slim went in town. Say, you seen Lennie?

CROOKS. You mean the big guy?

CANDY. Yes. Seen him around any place?

CROOKS. (*Goes back to his bunk, sits down, says shortly.*) He's in here.

CANDY. (*Stands in doorway, scratching wrist. Makes no attempt to enter.*) Look, Lennie, I been figuring something out. About the place.

CROOKS. (*Irritably.*) You can come in if you want.

CANDY. (*Embarrassed.*) I don't know. 'Course if you want me to.

CROOKS. Oh, come on in. Everybody's comin' in. You might just as well. Gettin' to be a goddamn race track. (*Tries to conceal his pleasure.*)

CANDY. (*Still embarrassed.*) You've got a nice cozy little place in here. Must be nice to have a room to yourself this way.

CROOKS. Sure. And a manure pile under the window. All to myself. It's swell.

LENNIE. (*Breaking in.*) You said about the place.

CANDY. You know, I been here a long time. An' Crooks been here a long time. This is the first time I ever been in his room.

CROOKS. (Darkly.) Guys don't come in a colored man's room. Nobody been here but Slim.

LENNIE. (Jrsistently.) The place. You said about the place.

CANDY. Yeah. I got it all figured out. We can make some real money on them rabbits if we go about it right.

LENNIE. But I get to tend 'em. George says I get to tend 'em. He promised.

CROOKS. (Brutally.) You guys is just kiddin' yourselves. You'll talk about it a hell of a lot, but you won't get no land. You'll be a swamper here until they take you out in a box. Hell, I seen too many guys.

CANDY. (Angrily.) We're gonna do it. George says we are. We got the money right now.

CROOKS. Yeah. And where is George now? In town in a cat-house. That's where your money's goin'. I tell you I seen it happen too many times.

CANDY. George ain't got the money in town. The money's in the bank. Me and Lennie and George. We gonna have a room to ourselves. We gonna have a dog and chickens. We gonna have green corn and maybe a cow.

CROOKS. (Jmpressed.) You say you got the money?

CANDY. We got most of it. Just a little bit more to get. Have it all in one month. George's got the land all picked out too.

CROOKS. (Exploring his spine with his hands.) I've never seen a guy really do it. I seen guys nearly crazy with loneliness for land, but every time a cat-house or a blackjack game took it away from 'em. (Hesitates, then speaks timidly.) If you guys would want a hand to work for nothin'—just his keep, why, I'd come and lend a hand. I ain't so crippled I can't work like a son-of-a-bitch if I wanted to.

GEORGE. (Strolls through door, hands in pockets, leans against wall, speaks in half-satiric, rather gentle voice.) You couldn't go to bed like I told you, could you, Lennie? Hell, no—you got to get out in society an' flap your mouth. Holdin' a convention out here.

LENNIE. (Defending himself.) You was gone. There wasn't nobody in the bunkhouse. I ain't done no bad things, George.

GEORGE. (Still casually.) Only time I get any peace is when you're

53

asleep. If you ever get walkin' in your sleep I'll chop off your head like a chicken. (*Chops with his hand.*)

CROOKS. (*Coming to* LENNIE'S *defense.*) We was jus' settin' here talkin'. Ain't no harm in that.

GEORGE. Yeah, I heard you. (*A weariness has settled on him.*) Got to be here ever' minute, I guess. Got to watch ya. (*To* CROOKS.) It ain't nothing against you, Crooks. We just wasn't gonna tell nobody.

CANDY. (*Tries to change subject.*) Didn't you have no fun in town?

GEORGE. Oh! I set in a chair and Susy was crackin' jokes an' the guys was startin' to raise a little puny hell. Christ Almighty—I never been this way before. I'm jus' gonna set out a dime and a nickel for a shot an' I think what a hell of a lot of bulk carrot seed you can get for fifteen cents.

CANDY. Not in them damn little envelopes—but bulk seed—you sure can.

GEORGE. So purty soon I come back. I can't think of nothing else. Them guys slingin' money around got me jumpy.

CANDY. Guy got to have *some* fun. I was to a parlor house in Bakersfield once. God Almighty, what a place. Went upstairs on a red carpet. They was big pitchers on the wall. We set in big sof' chairs. They was cigarettes on the table—an' they was *free*. Purty soon a Jap come in with drinks on a tray an' them *drinks* was free. Take all you want. (*In a reverie.*) Purty soon the girls come in an' they was jus' as polite an' nice an' quiet an' purty. Didn't seem like hookers. Made ya kinda scared to ask 'em. . . . That was a long time ago.

GEORGE. Yeah? An' what'd them sof' chairs set you back?

CANDY. Fifteen bucks.

GEORGE. (*Scornfully.*) So ya got a cigarette an' a whiskey an' a look at a purty dress an' it cost ya twelve and a half bucks extra. You shot a week's pay to walk on that red carpet.

CANDY. (*Still entranced with his memory.*) A week's pay? Sure. But I worked weeks all my life. I can't remember none of them weeks. But . . . that was nearly twenty years ago. And I can remember that. Girl I went with was named Arline. Had on a pink silk dress.

GEORGE. (*Turns suddenly and looks out door into the dark barn,*

54

speaks savagely.) I s'pose ya lookin' for Curley? (CURLEY'S WIFE *appears in door.*) Well, Curley ain't here.

CURLEY'S WIFE. (*Determined now.*) I know Curley ain't here. I wanted to ast Crooks somepin'. I didn't know you guys was here.

CANDY. Didn't George tell you before—we don't want nothing to do with you. You know damn well Curley ain't here.

CURLEY'S WIFE. I know where Curley went. Got his arm in a sling an' he went anyhow. I tell ya I come out to ast Crooks somepin'.

CROOKS. (*Apprehensively.*) Maybe you better go along to your own house. You hadn't ought to come near a colored man's room. I don't want no trouble. You don't want to ask me nothing.

CANDY. (*Rubbing his wrist stump.*) You got a husband. You got no call to come foolin' around with other guys, causin' trouble.

CURLEY'S WIFE. (*Suddenly angry.*) I try to be nice an' polite to you lousy bindle bums—but you're too good. I tell ya I could of went with shows. An'—an' a guy wanted to put me in pitchers right in Hollywood. (*Looks about to see how she is impressing them. Their eyes are hard.*) I come out here to ast somebody somepin' an' ——

CANDY. (*Stands up suddenly, knocks nail keg over backward, speaks angrily.*) I had enough. You ain't wanted here. We tole you you ain't. Callin' us bindle stiffs. You got floozy idears what us guys amounts to. You ain't got sense enough to see us guys ain't bindle stiffs. S'pose you could get us *canned*—s'pose you *could.* You think we'd hit the highway an' look for another two-bit job. You don't know we got our own ranch to go to an' our own house an' fruit trees. An' we got friends. That's what we got. Maybe they was a time when we didn't have nothing, but that ain't so no more.

CURLEY'S WIFE. You damn ol' goat. If you had two bits, you'd be in Soledad gettin' a drink an' suckin' the bottom of the glass.

GEORGE. Maybe she could ask Crooks what she come to ask an' then get the hell home. I don't think she come to ask nothing.

CURLEY'S WIFE. What happened to Curley's hand? (CROOKS *laughs.* GEORGE *tries to shut him up.*) So it wasn't no machine. Curley didn't act like he was tellin' the truth. Come on, Crooks—what happened?

CROOKS. I wasn't there. I didn't see it.

CURLEY'S WIFE. (*Eagerly.*) What happened? I won't let on to

55

Curley. He says he caught his han' in a gear. (CROOKS *is silent.*) Who done it?

GEORGE. Didn't nobody do it.

CURLEY'S WIFE. (*Turns slowly to* GEORGE.) So *you* done it. Well, he had it comin'.

GEORGE. I didn't have no fuss with Curley.

CURLEY'S WIFE. (*Steps near him, smiling.*) Maybe now you ain't scared of him no more. Maybe you'll talk to me sometimes now. Ever'body was scared of him.

GEORGE. (*Speaks rather kindly.*) Look! I didn't sock Curley. If he had trouble, it ain't none of our affair. Ask Curley about it. Now listen. I'm gonna try to tell ya. We tole you to get the hell out and it don't do no good. So I'm gonna tell you another way. Us guys got somepin' we're gonna do. If you stick around you'll gum up the works. It ain't your fault. If a guy steps on a round pebble an' falls down an' breaks his neck, it ain't the pebble's fault, but the guy wouldn't of did it if the pebble wasn't there.

CURLEY'S WIFE. (*Puzzled.*) What you talkin' about pebbles? If you didn't sock Curley, who did? (*Looks at others, then steps quickly over to* LENNIE.) Where'd you get them bruises on your face?

GEORGE. I tell you he got his hand caught in a machine.

LENNIE. (*Looks anxiously at* GEORGE, *miserably.*) He caught his han' in a machine.

GEORGE. So now get out of here.

CURLEY'S WIFE. (*Goes close to* LENNIE, *speaks softly, note of affection in her voice.*) So . . . it was you. Well . . . maybe you're dumb like they say . . . an' maybe . . . you're the only guy on the ranch with guts. (*Puts hand on* LENNIE'S *shoulder. He looks up in her face and a smile grows on his face. She strokes his shoulder.*) You're a nice fella.

GEORGE. (*Suddenly leaps at her ferociously, grabs her shoulder and whirls her around.*) Listen . . . you! I tried to give you a break. Don't you walk into nothing! We ain't gonna let you mess up what we're gonna do. You let this guy alone an' get the hell out of here.

CURLEY'S WIFE. (*Defiant but slightly frightened.*) You ain't tellin' me what to do. (BOSS *appears in door, stands legs spread, thumbs hooked over his belt.*) I got a right to talk to anybody I want to.

GEORGE. Why, you —— (GEORGE, *furious, steps close—hand is*

raised to strike her. She cowers a little. GEORGE *stiffens, seeing* BOSS, *frozen in position. Others see* BOSS, *too. She retreats slowly.* GEORGE'S *hand drops slowly to his side—he takes two slow backward steps. Hold the scene for a moment.*)

CURTAIN

ACT III

SCENE 1

Mid-afternoon Sunday.

One end of interior of barn. Backstage the hay slopes up sharply against the wall. High in upstage wall a large hay window. On each side are seen hay racks, behind which are the stalls with horses in them. Throughout this scene the horses can be heard in their stalls, rattling their halter chains and chewing at the hay. The entrance is down R. The boards of the barn are not close together. Streaks of afternoon sun come between them, made visible by dust in the air. From outside comes the clang of horseshoes on the playing peg, shouts of men encouraging or jeering. In the barn there is a feeling of quiet and humming and lazy warmth.

Curtain rises on LENNIE *sitting in the hay, looking down at a little dead puppy in front of him. Puts out hand and strokes it clear from one end to the other.*[1]

LENNIE. (*Softly.*) Why do you got to get killed? You ain't so little as mice. I didn't bounce you hard. (*Bends pup's head up and looks in its face.*) Now maybe George ain't gonna let me tend no rabbits if he finds out you got killed. (*Scoops a little hollow and lays the puppy in it out of sight and covers it over with hay. He stares at the mound he has made.*) This ain't no bad thing like I got to hide in the brush. I'll tell George I found it dead. (*Unburies pup and inspects it. Twists its ears and works his fingers in its fur. Sorrowfully.*) But he'll know. George always knows. He'll say: "You done it. Don't try to put nothin' over on me." And he'll say: "Now just for that you don't get to tend no—you-know-whats." (*His anger rises. Addresses pup.*) God damn you. Why do you got to get killed? You ain't so little as mice. (*Picks up pup and hurls it from him, turns his back on it. Sits bent over his knees, moaning to himself.*) Now he won't let me. . . . **Now he**

[1] See p. 5, Production Note.

won't let me. (*Outside a clang of horseshoes on iron stake and a little chorus of cries.* LENNIE *gets up and brings pup back and lays it in the hay and sits down. He mourns.*) You wasn't big enough. They tole me and tole me you wasn't. I didn't know you'd get killed so easy. Maybe George won't care. This here goddamn little son-of-a-bitch wasn't nothin' to George.

CANDY. (*Voice from behind stalls.*) Lennie, where you at? (LENNIE *frantically buries pup under hay.* CANDY *enters excitedly.*) Thought I'd find ya here. Say . . . I been talkin' to Slim. It's okay. We ain't gonna get the can. Slim been talkin' to the boss. Slim tol' the boss you guys is good buckers. The boss got to move that grain. 'Member what hell the boss give us las' night? He tol' Slim he got his eye on you an' George. But you ain't gonna get the can. Oh! an' say. The boss give Curley's wife hell, too. Tole her never to go near the men no more. Give her worse hell than you an' George. (*For first time notices* LENNIE'S *dejection.*) Ain't you glad?

LENNIE. Sure

CANDY. You ain't sick?

LENNIE. Uh-uh!

CANDY. I got to go tell George. See you later. (*Exits.* LENNIE, *alone, uncovers pup. Lies down in hay and sinks deep in it. Puts pup on his arm, strokes it.* CURLEY'S WIFE *enters secretly. A little mound of hay conceals* LENNIE *from her. She carries a small suitcase, very cheap. Crosses barn, buries case in hay. Stands up and looks to see whether it can be seen.* LENNIE, *watching her quietly, tries to cover pup with hay. She sees movement.*)

CURLEY'S WIFE. What—what you doin' here?

LENNIE. (*Sullenly.*) Jus' settin' here.

CURLEY'S WIFE. You seen what I done

LENNIE. Yeah! You brang a valise.

CURLEY'S WIFE. (*Comes near to him.*) You won't tell—will you?

LENNIE. (*Still sullen.*) I ain't gonna have nothing to do with you. George tole me. I ain't to talk to you or nothing. (*Covers pup a little more.*)

CURLEY'S WIFE. George give you *all* your orders?

LENNIE. Not talk nor nothing.

CURLEY'S WIFE. You won't tell about that suitcase? I ain't gonna stay here no more. Tonight I'm gonna get out. Come here an' get my stuff an' get out. I ain't gonna be run over no more. I'm gonna go in pitchers. (*Sees* LENNIE'S *hand stroking pup under hay.*) What you got there?

LENNIE. Nuthing. I ain't gonna talk to you. George says I ain't.

CURLEY'S WIFE. Listen: The guys got a horseshoe tenement out there. It's on'y four o'clock. Them guys ain't gonna leave that tenement. They got money bet. You don't need to be scared to talk to me.

LENNIE. (*Weakening a little.*) I ain't supposed to.

CURLEY'S WIFE. (*Watching his buried hand.*) What you got under there?

LENNIE. (*His woe comes back to him.*) Jus' my pup. Jus' my little ol' pup. (*Sweeps hay aside.*)

CURLEY'S WIFE. Why! He's dead.

LENNIE. (*Explaining sadly.*) He was so little. I was jus' playin' with him—an' he made like he's gonna bite me—an' I made like I'm gonna smack him—an'—I done it. An' then he was dead.

CURLEY'S WIFE. (*Consolingly.*) Don't you worry none. He was just a mutt. The whole country is full of mutts.

LENNIE. It ain't that so much. George gonna be mad. Maybe he won't let me—what he said I could tend.

CURLEY'S WIFE. (*Sits down in hay beside him, speaks soothingly.*) Don't you worry. Them guys got money bet on that horseshoe tenement. They ain't gonna leave it. And tomorra I'll be gone. I ain't gonna let them run over me. (*In following scene it is apparent that neither is listening to the other and yet as it goes on, as a happy tone increases, it can be seen that they are growing closer together.*)

LENNIE. We gonna have a little place an' raspberry bushes.

CURLEY'S WIFE. I ain't meant to live like this. I come from Salinas. Well, a show come through an' I talked to a guy that was in it. He says I could go with the show. My ol' lady wouldn't let me, 'cause I was on'y fifteen. I wouldn't be no place like this if I had went with that show, you bet.

LENNIE. Gonna take a sack an' fill it up with alfalfa an' ——

CURLEY'S WIFE. (*Hurrying on.*) 'Nother time I met a guy an' he was in pitchers. Went out to the Riverside Dance Palace with him. He said he was gonna put me in pitchers. Says I was a natural. Soon's he got back to Hollywood he was gonna write me about it. (*Looks impressively at* LENNIE.) I never got that letter. I think my ol' lady stole it. Well I wasn't gonna stay no place where they stole your letters. So I married Curley. Met *him* out to the Riverside Dance Palace too.

LENNIE. I hope George ain't gonna be mad about this pup.

CURLEY'S WIFE. I ain't tol' this to nobody before. Maybe I oughtn't to. I don't like Curley. He ain't a nice fella. I might a stayed with him but last night him an' his ol' man both lit into me. I don't have to stay here. (*Moves closer and speaks confidentially.*) Don't tell nobody till I get clear away. I'll go in the night an' thumb a ride to Hollywood.

LENNIE. We gonna get out a here purty soon. This ain't no nice place.

CURLEY'S WIFE. (*Ecstatically.*) Gonna get in the movies an' have nice clothes—all them nice clothes like they wear. An' I'll set in them big hotels and they'll take pitchers of me. When they have them openings I'll go an' talk in the radio . . . an' it won't cost me nothing 'cause I'm in the pitcher. (*Puts hand on* LENNIE'S *arm for a moment.*) All them nice clothes like they wear . . . because this guy says I'm a natural.

LENNIE. We gonna go way . . . far away from here.

CURLEY'S WIFE. 'Course, when I run away from Curley, my ol' lady won't never speak to me no more. She'll think I ain't decent. That's what she'll say. (*Defiantly.*) Well, we really ain't decent, no matter how much my ol' lady tries to hide it. My ol' man was a drunk. They put him away. There! Now I told.

LENNIE. George an' me was to the Sacramento Fair. One time I fell in the river an' George pulled me out an' saved me, an' then we went to the Fair. They got all kinds of stuff there. We seen long-hair rabbits.

CURLEY'S WIFE. My ol' man was a sign-painter when he worked. He used to get drunk an' paint crazy pitchers an' waste paint. One night when I was a little kid, him an' my ol' lady had an awful fight. They was always fightin'. In the middle of the night he come into my room, and he says, " I can't stand this no more. Let's you an' me go away." I guess he was drunk. (*Her voice takes on a curious wondering tenderness.*) I remember in the night—walkin' down the road, and the trees was black. I was pretty sleepy. He picked me up, an' he carried me on his back. He says, " We gonna live together. We gonna live together because you're my own little girl, an' not no stranger. No arguin' and fightin'," he says, " because you're my little daughter." (*Her*

61

voice becomes soft.) He says, " Why, you'll bake little cakes for me, an' I'll paint pretty pitchers all over the wall." (*Sadly.*) In the morning they caught us . . . an' they put him away. (*Pause.*) I wish we'd 'a' went.

LENNIE. Maybe if I took this here pup an' throwed him away George wouldn't never know.

CURLEY'S WIFE. They locked him up for a drunk, and in a little while he died.

LENNIE. Then maybe I could tend the rabbits without no trouble.

CURLEY'S WIFE. Don't you think of nothing but rabbits? (*Sound of horseshoe on metal.*) Somebody made a ringer.

LENNIE. (*Patiently.*) We gonna have a house and a garden, an' a place for alfalfa. And I take a sack and get it all full of alfalfa, and then I take it to the rabbits.

CURLEY'S WIFE. What makes you so nuts about rabbits?

LENNIE. (*Moves close to her.*) I like to pet nice things. Once at a fair I seen some of them long-hair rabbits. And they was nice, you bet. (*Despairingly.*) I'd even pet mice, but not when I could get nothin' better.

CURLEY'S WIFE. (*Giggles.*) I think you're nuts.

LENNIE. (*Earnestly.*) No, I ain't. George says I ain't. I like to pet nice things with my fingers. Soft things.

CURLEY'S WIFE. Well, who don't? Everybody likes that. I like to feel silk and velvet. You like to feel velvet?

LENNIE. (*Chuckling with pleasure.*) You bet, by God. And I had some too. A lady give me some. And that lady was—my Aunt Clara. She give it right to me. . . . (*Measuring with his hands.*) 'Bout this big a piece. I wisht I had that velvet right now. (*He frowns.*) I lost it. I ain't seen it for a long time.

CURLEY'S WIFE. (*Laughing.*) You're nuts. But you're a kinda nice fella. Jus' like a big baby. A person can see kinda what you mean. When I'm doin' my hair sometimes I jus' set there and stroke it, because it's so soft. (*Runs her fingers over top of her head.*) Some people got kinda coarse hair. You take Curley, his hair's just like wire. But mine is soft and fine. Here, feel. Right here. (*Takes LENNIE's hand and puts it on her head.*) Feel there and see how soft it is. (LENNIE's *fingers fall to stroking her hair.*) Don't you muss it up.

LENNIE. Oh, that's nice. (*Strokes harder.*) Oh, that's nice.

CURLEY'S WIFE. Look out now, you'll muss it. (*Angrily.*) You stop it now, you'll mess it all up. (*She jerks her head sideways and* LENNIE'S *fingers close on her hair and hang on. In a panic.*) Let go. (*Screams.*) You let go. (*Screams again. His other hand closes over her mouth and nose.*)

LENNIE. (*Begging.*) Oh, please don't do that. George'll be mad. (*She struggles violently to be free. A soft screaming comes from under* LENNIE'S *hand. Crying with fright.*) Oh, please don't do none of that. George gonna say I done a bad thing. (*He raises his hand from her mouth and a hoarse cry escapes. Angrily.*) Now don't. I don't want you to yell. You gonna get me in trouble just like George says you will. Now don't you do that. (*She struggles more.*) Don't you go yellin'. (*He shakes her violently. Her neck snaps sideways and she lies still. Looks down at her, cautiously removes his hand from over her mouth.*) I don't wanta hurt you. But George will be mad if you yell. (*When she doesn't answer he bends closely over her. Lifts her arm and lets it drop. For a moment he seems bewildered.*) I done a bad thing. I done another bad thing. (*He paws up the hay until it partly covers her. Sound of the horseshoe game comes from outside. And for the first time* LENNIE *seems conscious of it. He crouches down and listens.*) Oh, I done a real bad thing. I shouldn't 'a' did that. George will be mad. And . . . he said . . . and hide in the brush till he comes. . . . He's gonna be mad . . . in the brush till he comes. That's what he said. (*Picks up the puppy from beside the girl.*) I'll throw him away. It's bad enough like it is. (*Puts pup under his coat, creeps to wall, peers out between cracks, then creeps around to end of manger and disappears. Stage is vacant except for* CURLEY'S WIFE. *She lies in the hay half covered up, and looks very young and peaceful. Her rouged cheeks and red lips make her seem alive and sleeping lightly. For a moment the stage is absolutely silent. Then the horses stamp on other side of feeding rack. Halter chains clink and from outside men's voices come loud and clear.*)

CANDY. (*Offstage.*) Lennie! Oh, Lennie, you in there? (*He enters.*) I been figurin' some more, Lennie. Tell you what we can do. (*Sees* CURLEY'S WIFE, *stops. Rubs his whiskers.*) I didn't know you was here. You was tol' not to be here. (*Steps near her.*) You oughtn't to sleep out here. (*He is right beside her, looks down.*) Oh, Jesus Christ! (*Goes to door, calls softly.*) George, George! Come here . . . George!

63

GEORGE. (*Enters.*) What do you want?

CANDY. (*Points at* CURLEY'S WIFE.) Look.

GEORGE. What's the matter with her? (*Steps up beside her.*) Oh, Jesus Christ! (*Kneels beside her, feels her heart and wrist. Finally stands up slowly and stiffly. Through rest of scene* GEORGE *is wooden.*)

CANDY. What done it?

GEORGE. (*Coldly.*) Ain't you got any idea? (CANDY *looks away.*) I should of knew. I guess way back in my head I did.

CANDY. What we gonna do now, George? What we gonna do now?

GEORGE. (*Answering slowly and dully.*) Guess . . . we gotta . . . tell . . . the guys. Guess we got to catch him and lock him up. We can't let him get away. Why, the poor bastard would starve. (*Tries to reassure himself.*) Maybe they'll lock him up and be nice to him.

CANDY. (*Excitedly.*) You know better'n that, George. You know Curley's gonna want to get him lynched. You know how Curley is.

GEORGE. Yeah. . . . Yeah . . . that's right. I know Curley. And the other guys too. (*Looks back at* CURLEY'S WIFE.)

CANDY. (*Pleadingly.*) You and me can get that little place, can't we, George? You and me can go there and live nice, can't we? Can't we? (CANDY *drops his head and looks down at hay to indicate that he knows.*)

GEORGE. (*Shakes head slowly.*) It was somethin' me and him had. (*Softly.*) I think I knowed it from the very first. I think I knowed we'd never do her. He used to like to hear about it so much. I got fooled to thinkin' maybe we would. (CANDY *starts to speak but doesn't.* GEORGE, *as though repeating a lesson.*) I'll work my month and then I'll take my fifty bucks. I'll stay all night in some lousy cat-house or I'll set in a pool room until everybody goes home. An' then—I'll come back an' work another month. And then I'll have fifty bucks more.

CANDY. He's such a nice fellow. I didn't think he'd 'a' done nothing like this.

GEORGE. (*Gets grip on himself, straightens shoulders.*) Now listen. We gotta tell the guys. I guess they've gotta bring him in. They ain't no way out. Maybe they won't hurt him. I ain't gonna let 'em hurt Lennie. (*Sharply.*) Now you listen. The guys might think I was in on it. I'm gonna go in the bunkhouse. Then in a minute you come out and yell like you just seen her. Will you do that? So the guys won't think I was in on it?

CANDY. Sure, George. Sure, I'll do that.

GEORGE. Okay. Give me a couple of minutes then. And then you yell your head off. I'm goin' now. (GEORGE *exits.*)

CANDY. (*Watches him go, looks helplessly back at* CURLEY'S WIFE; *next words are in sorrow and anger.*) You goddamn tramp! You done it, didn't you? Everybody knowed you'd mess things up. You just wasn't no good. (*His voice shakes.*) I could of hoed in the garden and washed dishes for them guys. . . . (*Pauses a moment, then goes into a sing-song repeating the old words.*) If there was a circus or a baseball game . . . we would o' went to her . . . just said to hell with work and went to her. And they'd been a pig and chickens . . . and in the winter a little fat stove. An' us jus' settin' there . . . settin' there. . . . (*His eyes blind with tears, goes weakly to entrance of barn. Tries for a moment to break a shout out of his throat before he succeeds.*) Hey, you guys! Come here! Come here! (*Outside the noise of game stops. Sound of discussion and then voices come closer:* "What's the matter?" . . . "Who's that?" . . . "It's Candy." . . . "Something must have happened." *Enter* SLIM *and* CARLSON, YOUNG WHIT *and* CURLEY, CROOKS *in the back, keeping out of attention range. And last of all* GEORGE, *who has put on his blue denim coat and buttoned it. His black hat is pulled down low over his eyes.* "What's the matter?" . . . "What's happened?" *A gesture from* CANDY. *The men stare at* CURLEY'S WIFE. SLIM *goes to her, feels her wrist and touches her cheek with his fingers. His hand goes under her slightly twisted neck.* CURLEY *comes near. For a moment he seems shocked. Looks around helplessly, and suddenly comes to life.*)

CURLEY. I know who done it. That big son-of-a-bitch done it. I know he done it. Why, everybody else was out there playing horseshoes. (*Working himself into a fury.*) I'm gonna get him. I'm gonna get my shotgun. Why, I'll kill the big son-of-a-bitch myself. I'll shoot him in the guts. Come on, you guys. (*Runs out of barn.*)

CARLSON. I'll go get my Luger. (*Runs out, too.*)

SLIM. (*Quietly to* GEORGE.) I guess Lennie done it all right. Her neck's busted. Lennie could o' did that. (GEORGE *nods slowly.*

Half-questioning.) Maybe like that time in Weed you was tellin' me about. (GEORGE *nods. Gently.*) Well, I guess we got to get him. Where you think he might o' went?

GEORGE. (*Struggling to get words out.*) I don't know.

SLIM. I guess we gotta get him.

GEORGE. (*Stepping close, speaking passionately.*) Couldn't we maybe bring him in and lock him up? He's nuts, Slim, he never done this to be mean.

SLIM. If we could only keep Curley in. But Curley wants to shoot him. (*He thinks.*) And s'pose they lock him up, George, and strap him down and put him in a cage, that ain't no good.

GEORGE. I know. I know.

SLIM. I think there's only one way to get him out of it.

GEORGE. I know.

CARLSON. (*Enters running.*) The bastard stole my Luger. It ain't in my bag.

CURLEY. (*Enters carrying shotgun in his good hand. Officiously.*) All right, you guys. The nigger's got a shotgun. You take it, Carlson.

WHIT. Only cover around here is down by the river. He might have went there.

CURLEY. Don't give him no chance. Shoot for his guts, that'll double him over.

WHIT. I ain't got a gun.

CURLEY. Go in and tell my old man. Get a gun from him. Let's go now. (*Turns suspiciously on* GEORGE.) You're comin' with us, fella!

GEORGE. Yeah. I'll come. But listen, Curley, the poor bastard's nuts. Don't shoot him, he didn't know what he was doin'.

CURLEY. Don't shoot him! He's got Carlson's Luger, ain't he?

GEORGE. (*Weakly.*) Maybe Carlson lost his gun.

CARLSON. I seen it this morning. It's been took.

SLIM. (*Looking down at* CURLEY'S WIFE.) Curley, maybe you better stay here with your wife. (*Light is fading into evening.* CURLEY *hesitates. Seems almost to weaken, then hardens again.*)

CURLEY. Naw, I'm gonna shoot the guts out of that big bastard, I'm gonna get him myself. Come on, you guys.

SLIM. (*to* CANDY.) You stay here then, Candy. The rest of us better get goin'. (*They walk out,* SLIM *and* GEORGE *last. Exeunt*

all but CANDY, *who squats in the bay, watching the face of* CUR-
LEY'S WIFE.)
CANDY. Poor bastard.

CURTAIN

ACT III

SCENE 2

Evening.
The river bank again as in Act J—Scene 1.[1] Light from
the setting sun shines on the low brown hills. Among the
trees by the river, the shade is deep with evening feeling.
Sounds: distant barking of dogs and the quiet call of
quail.
Curtain rises on an empty stage. There is a sudden
whistle of evening wind that stirs the trees and scuds
the leaves on the ground. Stage is still again. LENNIE
enters as silently as a bear. He is bent over and wary.
On stage he looks behind him. Then takes from under
his coat the dead pup, lays it on the ground and, going
to the river, lies on his stomach and drinks. Returns to
dead pup, sits down beside it.

LENNIE. George gonna give me hell . . . I bet. I . . . won't tell
him. I'll bury him. (*Begins to scoop hole in sand in front of him.*
Softly.) But I didn't forget, you bet. I come right here. Hide in
the brush an' wait for George. (*Works carefully at his little grave,*
shaping hole. At last he picks up pup and lays it in hole. Mourn-
ing.) He gonna give me hell. He gonna wish he was alone. (*Ad-*
justs pup in hole, turning it around to make it fit better. Defiantly.)
Well . . . I can go right up in the hills an' find a cave. 'Course
I wouldn't never have no ketchup. (*Begins packing sand down*
carefully about pup, patting it in beat with his words.) I'll—go—
away—go—away. (*Every word a pat. Fills grave carefully,*
smooths sand over it.) There now. (*Gathers leaves and scatters*
them over the place. Gets up on his knees, cocks his head to in-
spect job.) Now. I won't never tell George. (*Sinks back to sit-*
ting position.) He'll know. He always knows. (*Far off sound of*

[1] See p. 5, *Production Note.*

voices approaching. They come closer during the scene. Suddenly the clicking warning of a cock-quail, then the drum of the flock's wings. GEORGE *enters silently, but hurriedly.*)

GEORGE. (*In hoarse whisper.*) Get in the tules—quick.

LENNIE. I ain't done nothing, George. (*Voices are very close.*)

GEORGE. (*Frantically.*) Get in the tules—damn you. (Voices are *nearly there.* GEORGE *half pushes* LENNIE *down among tules. The tops rustle showing his crawling progress.*)

WHIT. (*Offstage.*) There's George. (*Enters.*) Better not get so far ahead. You ain't got a gun. (*Enter* SLIM, CARLSON, BOSS, CURLEY, *and three other ranch hands, armed with shotguns and rifles.*)

CARLSON. He musta come this way. Them prints in the sand was aimed this way.

SLIM. (*Has been regarding* GEORGE..) Now look. We ain't gonna find him stickin' in a bunch this way. We got to spread out.

CURLEY. Brush is pretty thick here. He might be lying in the brush. (*Steps toward tules.* GEORGE *moves quickly after him.*)

SLIM. (*Seeing the move, speaks quickly.*) Look. (*Squinting.*) Up there's the country road an' open fields an' over there's the highway. Let's spread out an' cover the brush.

BOSS. Slim's right. We got to spread.

SLIM. We better drag up to the roads an' then drag back.

CURLEY. 'Member what I said—shoot for his guts.

SLIM. Okay, move out. Me an' George'll go up to the country road. You guys gets the highway an' drag back.

BOSS. If we get separated, we'll meet here. Remember this place.

CURLEY. All I care is getting the bastard. (*Men move off* R., *talking.* SLIM *and* GEORGE *move slowly upstage, listening to voices that grow fainter and fainter.*)

SLIM. (*Softly to* GEORGE.) Where is he? (GEORGE *looks at him in the eyes for a long moment. Finally trusts him and points with his thumb toward tules.*) You want—I should—go away? (GEORGE *nods slowly, looking at ground.* SLIM *starts away, comes back, tries to say something, instead puts hand on* GEORGE'S *shoulder for a second, then hurries off upstage.*)

GEORGE. (*Moves woodenly toward bank and tule clump, sits down.*) Lennie! (*Tules shiver again and* LENNIE *emerges dripping.*)

LENNIE. Where's them guys goin'? (*Long pause.*)

GEORGE. Huntin'.

LENNIE. Whyn't we go with 'em? I like huntin'. (*Waits for an-*

swer. GEORGE *stares across river.*) Is it 'cause I done a bad thing?

GEORGE. It don't make no difference.

LENNIE. Is that why we can't go huntin' with them guys?

GEORGE. (*Woodenly.*) It don't make no difference. . . . Sit down, Lennie. Right there. (*Light is going now. In distance are shouts of men.* GEORGE *turns head and listens.*)

LENNIE. George!

GEORGE. Yeah?

LENNIE. Ain't you gonna give me hell?

GEORGE. Give ya hell?

LENNIE. Sure. . . . Like you always done before. Like—"If I didn' have you I'd take my fifty bucks . . ."

GEORGE. (*Softly as if in wonder.*) Jesus Christ, Lennie, you can't remember nothing that happens. But you remember every word I say!

LENNIE. Well, ain't you gonna say it?

GEORGE. (*Reciting.*) "If I was alone I—could live—so easy. (*His voice is monotonous.*) I could get a job and not have no mess . . ."

LENNIE. Go on, go on! "And when the end of the month come . . ."

GEORGE. "And when the end of the month come, I could take my fifty bucks and go to—a cat-house. . . ."

LENNIE. (*Eagerly.*) Go on, George, ain't you gonna give me no more hell?

GEORGE. No!

LENNIE. I can go away. I'll go right off in the hills and find a cave if you don't want me.

GEORGE. (*Speaks as though his lips were stiff.*) No, I want you to stay here with me.

LENNIE. (*Craftily.*) Then tell me like you done before.

GEORGE. Tell you what?

LENNIE. 'Bout the other guys and about us!

GEORGE. (*Recites again.*) "Guys like us got no families. They got a little stake and then they blow it in. They ain't got nobody in the world that gives a hoot in hell about 'em!"

LENNIE. (*Happily.*) "But not *us.*" Tell about us now.

GEORGE. "But not us."

LENNIE. "Because . . ."

GEORGE. "Because I got you and . . ."

LENNIE. (*Triumphantly.*) "And I got you. We got each other,"

69

that's what, that gives a hoot in hell about us. (*A breeze blows up the leaves, then they settle back again. Shouts of men again. This time closer.*)

GEORGE. (*Takes off hat, shakily.*) Take off your hat, Lennie. The air feels fine!

LENNIE. (*Removes hat, lays it on ground in front of him.*) Tell how it's gonna be. (*Again sound of men.* GEORGE *listens.*)

GEORGE. Look acrost the river, Lennie, and I'll tell you like you can almost see it. (LENNIE *turns head, looks across river.*) " We gonna get a little place . . ." (*Reaches in side pocket, brings out* CARLSON'S *revolver. Hand and gun lie on ground behind* LENNIE'S *back. He stares at back of* LENNIE'S *head at the place where spine and skull are joined. Sounds of men's voices talking offstage.*)

LENNIE. Go on! (GEORGE *raises gun, but his hand shakes and he drops his hand on to the ground.*) Go on! How's it gonna be? " We gonna get a little place. . . ."

GEORGE. (*Thickly.*) " We'll have a cow. And we'll have maybe a pig and chickens—and down the flat we'll have a . . . little piece of alfalfa. . . ."

LENNIE. (*Shouting.*) " For the rabbits! "

GEORGE. " For the rabbits! "

LENNIE. " And I get to tend the rabbits? "

GEORGE. " And you get to tend the rabbits! "

LENNIE. (*Giggling with happiness.*) " And live on the fat o' the land! "

GEORGE. Yes. (LENNIE *turns his head. Quickly.*) Look over there, Lennie. Like you can really see it.

LENNIE. Where?

GEORGE. Right acrost that river there. Can't you almost see it?

LENNIE. (*Moving.*) Where, George?

GEORGE. It's over there. You keep lookin', Lennie. Just keep lookin'.

LENNIE. I'm lookin', George. I'm lookin'.

GEORGE. That's right. It's gonna be nice there. Ain't gonna be no trouble, no fights. Nobody ever gonna hurt nobody, or steal from 'em. It's gonna be—nice.

LENNIE. I can see it, George. I can see it! Right over there! I can see it! (GEORGE *fires.* LENNIE *crumples, falls behind the brush. Voices of men in distance.*)

CURTAIN

PROPERTY LIST

ACT I

2 blanket rolls
2 cans beans (full)
Opener
2 pocket-knives
(Over bunks): alarm clocks, soap,
   talc powder, razors, pulp magazines, medicine bottles, combs,
   neckties

Large push broom
Small yellow can
Leather wristband
2 slips paper
Time book and pencil
Rope for sheep dog
Deck of cards
Stetson hat

ACT II

Tin shaded electric light
Bull whip
Small puppy
Bag, Luger pistol inside (shell for
   gun)
Tools on working-bench
Broken and mended harness, etc.

Medicines in cans and bottles
Tattered books
Big alarm clock
Shotgun
Pair of rubber boots
Large pair of gold spectacles
2 empty nail kegs

ACT III

Dead puppy (fake)
Small cheap suitcase

Several shotguns and rifles

NEW PLAYS

• **TAKING SIDES by Ronald Harwood.** Based on the true story of one of the world's greatest conductors whose wartime decision to remain in Germany brought him under the scrutiny of a U.S. Army determined to prove him a Nazi. *"A brave, wise and deeply moving play delineating the confrontation between culture, and power, between art and politics, between irresponsible freedom and responsible compromise."* --London Sunday Times. [4M, 3W] ISBN: 0-8222-1566-7

• **MISSING/KISSING by John Patrick Shanley.** Two biting short comedies, MISSING MARISA and KISSING CHRISTINE, by one of America's foremost dramatists and the Academy Award winning author of *Moonstruck.* *" ... Shanley has an unusual talent for situations ... and a sure gift for a kind of inner dialogue in which people talk their hearts as well as their minds...."* --N.Y. Post. MISSING MARISA [2M], KISSING CHRISTINE [1M, 2W] ISBN: 0-8222-1590-X

• **THE SISTERS ROSENSWEIG by Wendy Wasserstein, Pulitzer Prize-winning** author of *The Heidi Chronicles.* Winner of the 1993 Outer Critics Circle Award for Best Broadway Play. A captivating portrait of three disparate sisters reuniting after a lengthy separation on the eldest's 50th birthday. *"The laughter is all but continuous."* --New Yorker. *"Funny. Observant. A play with wit as well as acumen.... In dealing with social and cultural paradoxes, Ms. Wasserstein is, as always, the most astute of commentators."* --N.Y. Times. [4M, 4W] ISBN: 0-8222-1348-6

• **MASTER CLASS by Terrence McNally.** Winner of the 1996 Tony Award for Best Play. Only a year after winning the Tony Award for *Love! Valour! Compassion!,* Terrence McNally scores again with the most celebrated play of the year, an unforgettable portrait of Maria Callas, our century's greatest opera diva. *"One of the white-hot moments of contemporary theatre. A total triumph."* --N.Y. Post. *"Blazingly theatrical."* -- USA Today. [3M, 3W] ISBN: 0-8222-1521-7

• **DEALER'S CHOICE by Patrick Marber.** A weekly poker game pits a son addicted to gambling against his own father, who also has a problem but won't admit it. *"... make tracks to DEALER'S CHOICE, Patrick Marber's wonderfully masculine, razor-sharp dissection of poker-as-life.... It's a play that comes out swinging and never lets up -- a witty, wisecracking drama that relentlessly probes the tortured souls of its six very distinctive ... characters. CHOICE is a cutthroat pleasure that you won't want to miss."* --Time Out (New York). [6M] ISBN: 0-8222-1616-7

• **RIFF RAFF by Laurence Fishburne.** RIFF RAFF marks the playwriting debut of one of Hollywood's most exciting and versatile actors. *"Mr. Fishburne is surprisingly and effectively understated, with scalding bubbles of anxiety breaking through the surface of a numbed calm."* --N.Y. Times. *"Fishburne has a talent and a quality...[he] possesses one of the vital requirements of a playwright -- a good ear for the things people say and the way they say them."* --N.Y. Post. [3M] ISBN: 0-8222-1545-4

DRAMATISTS PLAY SERVICE, INC.
440 Park Avenue South, New York, NY 10016 212-683-8960 Fax 212-213-1539
postmaster@dramatists.com www.dramatists.com